Content

I hope you never cower from your dark chapters, but highlight them as proof of perseverance, endurance, and strength."

—Kierra C. T. Banks

The Bee Killer

Curt Rude

—Robert E. Lee *"It is well that war is so terrible, or we should grow too fond of it."*

Different day—Same oven. Scorching heat, Kabul style. The sun, a blood splat, rose. Soldiers repositioned in disappearing shadows. Night-vision goggles had transformed them into patriotic vampires in the service of Uncle Sam. The enemy couldn't shoot what they couldn't see. Great plan until the ride no-showed. Three of the soldiers wore scars from Muslim bullets. Seven had pulled messed up bodies to choppers. Nick and Butternut were newbies. They still thought death came for others. Drill Sergeant told 'em to use their training to stay alive. It was the unexpected stuff scared Nick the most. He worked himself up from a crouch and unzipped. Everyone heard him splashing the dust into a mud-puddle.

"Jeez ... can't believe I hada take a leak."

"Don't worry about it; first time oudda the wire. Piss in the moonlight; shoot in the sunlight. You gotta get your blood type marked on your boots. Then let's make sure you got a dog tag around the neck and one on the boot. Little things keep your ass unrefrigerated."

O'Connor liked the kid. He was older than O'Connor but he'd be a kid—Nicky-New-Guy—until he was baptized with bad intentions. War gore splattered on the ol' face usually did the trick: urban renewal for the soul. No room for kindness.

The pick-up point was half a block north. Plan called for a ride back to chow and shut-eye. If no ride showed before the darkness vanished, it could get bad. He glanced at the other eleven infidels muttering—"fuck".

Sarge was thinking. Mission had required one bomb-maker to be put out of business, and Military Intelligence fingered the Islamic rat and the hole he called home. Things had gotten nasty when they kicked a door and found no rodent, just women undressed enough to really piss-off the homeowner. The soldiers had bolted for their ride with the gentleman shaking his fist at them; Muslims killed male eyes peeking at their women. O'Connor squeezed his ankle. He figured a medic could take his pulse through his boot. Kabul doors usually gave before bone; but not this time.

"Yo Connor. My man. That some kick. You A-okay in my book dog."

Tee Pee stared through O'Connor. Shee'it … that low life A-rab didn't know shit from Allah for a sec," Tee Pee chuckled. "All I'm a-sayin' is ya did good."

2

O'Connor put weight on his foot. Pain put the brakes on talking. "Damn ride would be nice. This leg killin' me."

"Ah hell … you see that Mu-se-lum? He hada look o' pure surprise under that beard. Yessirree." Tee Pee started singing, "Been in the desert ona camel got no name, it felt good to be—" A voice groaned for Tee Pee to shut it.

Pain pulled O'Connor's mouth into a tight line. "Jesus … we should write them words down. Sing your way onto American Idol. You gonna remember me, pal … when you're one of those people?"

"Beggin' your pardon, Connor. I ain't never forgettin' yo' white ass. I'm a feelin' it in my bones though. Damn too quiet for my taste. Natives fixin' to make things interestin'." He looked at the windows. "You kick the doh good though … You know how it is … can't give the infidels wood. Hell, I'm not so sure I could get mine up with a crane. This place just takes it out of ya. Now they riled some to the point I could hear a spider choken' ona sand flea a mile 'way. Ain't supposed to be this quiet atall—"

"Goddammit Tee Pee, shut it."

O'Connor thought it sounded like Hammer Mason. Thoughts were tiptoeing around on the nerves in his face. No kids saying 'Please only one dollar.' No ladies bobbing to the market wrapped

3

up like it was thirty-below. Nothing. Not even prayers being called for. Ahhh shit, we gonna get hit. "'Fraid you got it right … Tee Pee."

Nick was quiet. Butternut, the other new boot, stiffened. "Y'all serious? Reckon it's time to start puttin' holes in Diaper Heads." He pushed a lump of chew around in his mouth.

O'Connor studied him for bullshit. Fear did funny things to newbies: some became pale and wide eyed; others got red faced and goofy. Butternut acted like killing was more important than breathing. "You serious?"

Tee Pee glanced from O'Connor to Butternut. "Howeee … Butter-numb-nuts. You gots a gen-u-ine hatred, now don't you?"

"You got that right, Toilet Paper. I intend to waste Dune Coons. Told my granpaw and grandmama I'd show A-rabs what Americans made of; they more likeable when they dirt-napping." He pointed his weapon at buildings while tapping the trigger. "Way I see it … I'ma mudshark travel agent. Yes-er-ree … I intend to blast them glorified animals until they with seventy-two virgins."

Muthafucka? Who call me dat … Toilet Paper?"

"Everyone call you Tee Pee." Butternut said.

"Oh c'mon man, it's Tee Pee like what's the Indians lived in, for fuck's sake." Tee Pee shook his head.

"You good with math?" Tee Pee started clicking his safety off and on with each word spoken. "I mean, Butternut … ya can count—right? There be twelve of us. Let's say a hundred li'le Muhammads show up with noisemakers. Do thee math … that equals fucked for us. Now befo' the fun commences let's hear how you landed your little ol' nickname."

"Why, I am right proud of my name. I got me kinfolk who fought against northern aggression a-wearin' the butternut greys. They marched with Old Jack himself, Thomas Jackson as in Stonewall—"

"You got balls, I'll give ya dat … brains is what I'm wondering 'bout." Tee Pee shook his head. "Whewee … they go and let you out of the acorn bin so now it's our bidnis ta babyshit yo' ass."

Butternut pulled a sleeve across his face. He didn't want sweat finding his eyes when the shooting started. "I gauran-god-damn-tee-it, I came to shoot me some of them fellers in white dresses and sandals."

Nick whispered in O'Connor's direction. "Are we really gonna get it, Sir? Hit I mean."

"Hell, they never let on when they gonna hit us." O'Connor looked down at his weapon and rattled the magazine. "It reminds me of one badass surprise party. If ya wanna dance, ya gotta pay the fiddler. It's why we're here: to shoot and be shot. You know, it's kinda like dancing. They shoot once, we shoot twice, cha-cha-cha." He winked at Nick.

Nick spoke like he was just waking-up. "I got me a girl. Who knows, maybe a baby girl by now. I believed it all: Make America great again. Just work hard. I graduated and landed in a kitchen. I stayed around until the owner forgot to make me part owner. After I graduated, America turned into one big shit storm. Met a waitress there. Year o' school left and a baby on the way. A girl. Did I say that? I wanna do right for my girls."

"You have the right stuff to be a good daddy, Nick." O'Connor said.

Radio's always on in that kitchen and they talk about army strong and being one of the few and the proud. You never figure it'll come to this when you're with the recruiters." Nick glanced at Butternut making sure he wasn't listening. "Now I get the feelin' dyin' can happen … but how can I be a daddy if I'm dead?"

6

O'Connor hocked up a loogie and hit a rock almost five feet from where he crouched. "There … you see that? I hit what I spit and shoot at. I got your back. Nick, it comes down to being just a toss of the die. Shit, it's scarier stateside in a classroom than being in ahh Muslim Hoedown. I was a nice guy wanted to be a gym teacher in my former life. Then I jumped the pond and someone finds a skull. A human skull. He filled it with sand and then … know what we did with it?"

Nick shook his head no.

"We dug up some ribs outta the sand and started bowling. I mean, we busted ribs apart and stuck 'em in the sand and rolled that damn skull," O'Connor shook his head. "First ball I'd seen with dried chunks of hair and shit on it. Sick man." O'Connor scratched at his upper lip with his bottom teeth.

Nick stared at him.

"Around here … we shoot, we shovel and shut-up. We bury mistakes. Thinkers die. Shooters live. No worries. You'll catch on."

Nick cleared his throat. "I can shoot pretty good—"

Tee Pee looked over with a grin. "Time to serve 'em a little whoop ass. Done it befo' … do it aaa-gen'. Ain't that right, O'Connor? Shoot out at the Okay Muslim Corral."

7

Butternut held his carbine up and smiled with even, straight teeth; his orthodontist must've been proud. "Dead Muslims coming right-up."

A dog barked over metallic sounds. O'Connor hunkered down trying to figure it out. Then he spotted several bobbing heads carrying tubes on a roof to the east of their position: mortars! O'Connor lunged for the sergeant.

"Mortars, Sarge." Everyone heard this and it got quiet. "Number of 'em on the roof to the east, Sir."

"Let's go, Ladies!" the sergeant roared and sprang for an alley. Everyone heard the kah-chunk of a mortar. The shell hit the bricks O'Connor had just been hiding behind. One piece was driven into Butternut's face; everything from the nose down exploded to the side in a mangled mess. Tooth and bone pierced flesh, giving him a lamprey-like appearance. He stopped and touched the damage with his finger tips. He gurgled, "Gggaaaggga," and emptied a clip.

"Halt!" The sergeant motioned with his hand.

O'Connor ran into his back. "We need cover, Sarge."

"Lookit." A girl, eight or nine, struggled toward them with her hands out, crying. She was under a large backpack. Brown eyes said it all. She was terrified. Her presence confused the group. A

8

bearded man fired from behind her. Everyone hit the dirt. The sergeant spun around and hollered, "She's going off when we hit the alley!"

Bullets pocked the sand near his boots. The first mortar covered them in smoke and dirt. Butternut stood up and started pounding the buildings with his M4; his grandparents would have been proud.

Nick broke for the girl at a full sprint.

"Get your ass back here!" O'Connor screamed. "Goddammit, Nick, stop!" A brilliant flash of violence blinded everyone. As O'Connor looked up into Tee Pee's face, he realized he was on his back. He felt like he'd been in the sun without lotion. "Fuckin'-a," he coughed.

Tee Pee pulled him onto a shoulder and forced him to run-hop to cover. Their ride materialized at the end of the alley. The driver had spotted the mortar cloud and found them. Eleven soldiers dove into it, two lugging most of Nick's smoldering remains plopped them on the floor.

* * *

O'Connor wanted to sleep but his brain wasn't having it. His eyes felt like balls of sandpaper. Anytime he fell asleep Nicholas was waiting. O'Connor called it dream-sharing.

"Thought you had my back, Asshole," Nichols told O'Connor in one of their first get-togethers. Nicholas tried punching him in another dream but his arm had fallen off.

O'Connor was haunted by sleep. Drinking was the only thing kept Nicholas away.

"Gentleman Jack" on-the-rocks knocked him out and he had slept for almost three whole hours. His face had landed on a tabletop in the rec center. The others in the place had kept quiet, knowing he needed sleep.

He sat bolt upright with sweat dripping from his face. He didn't even recall what Nicholas had been up to. "Fuck, Dude," the only other soldier in the room told him, "the war's over. Let it go and don't go tellin' army shrinks. They can make shit downright bad for a guy can't let it go." He took the advice and ended up on a shuttle to the airport.

Dodging death and bullets made civilian life dull. His gun was gone and he felt naked to the point where he kept touching himself. Disarmed among strangers was not kosher.

Leaving Tee Pee back in the wild didn't work either.

O'Connor's leg had gotten him back into the tame place, but what about his buddies? No forgiving himself if shit happened to Tee Pee. He pulled a sleeve across his forehead and slouched in his chair. It was time to forget it all and let the good times roll.

Everyone seemed to walk around in slow-mo'. They would smile and say sorry way too much. Everyone one of 'em acted like they had no idea they were just blood pools waiting for bullets to cause leaks. O'Connor reminded himself these folks knew they were going to die but somehow had concluded it wasn't going to be today. He glanced at a couple carrying on at the counter. O'Connor inhaled and held his breath as if someone had just passed him an enormous joint. Once a stranger has designs on your life—as in wanting to shoot you into a chunk of meat— nothing in an airport is upsetting. All's good, he told himself as he slowly exhaled.

"Hey ... you were out like a light." The flabby girl had a square, pink face appearing much too small for the large balloon of a head it was planted on. She made grunty noises while licking ice cream from the corners of her smile.

"I was?" O'Connor was startled by the fact Nicholas let him catch some shuteye.

"Well now, where does a little girl get a snack around here? You know, Panda Express or something. I can leave these bags with you, can't I?"

O'Connor looked in both directions. "Don't know, but I'll watch your bag."

She had to be at least two axe handles wide, he guessed; she bulled into a crowd like a runaway boxcar parting a flock of pigeons.

A television toward the ceiling where she lumbered caught O'Connor's eye. Been awhile since he'd seen one. Sound was off on this one but words raced across the bottom of it. Another school shooting, car accident and a fire in Hawaii. He kept his eyes on the television hoping it would keep him awake. Then a commercial came on: bunch of soldiers somehow looking plenty happy. He caught it as it scrolled across the bottom of the screen. "When I'm asked what I'd done … Join the Team that makes a difference … The Army."

He knew there was no way in hell he'd made a difference killing goat-fuckers. He knew how the game was played: They debriefed him, took his weapon and kinda made polite talk. Stuff like if he knew how serious an offense it was to sneak arms into the States. Pretty obvious why. He had put an imaginary bullet into the

TV, he realized, while squeezing his finger on a trigger that wasn't there.

"You okay?" She licked one of her stubby fingers. "You musta really had a humdinger of a nightmare or something. You were sleepin' okay but rolling around that seat pretty good." She stared at him while squeezing the wrapper into a tight little ball. Sauce oozed out of the ball, necessitating some licking. "You'll be okay now you're awake. I should have saved you some of the egg-roll."

"No, I'm good."

"I'm Tonya."

"O'Connor, ma'am."

She pressed a book into her lap. "I picked this up in Hamburg." She licked the tip of her finger before flicking through about a quarter inch of pages. It was a red book with a bullet on it. The title included the word treason in it. "I'm just sooo captivated by the war. All these stories. Oh my, oh me. I'm just about done. It's yours then, Hon'." She smiled and began reading.

O'Connor stretched and rubbed his temple and looked around. So many people doing what they do: A lady pushing a stroller; he hadn't seen that for what seemed like a lifetime; a guy not old enough to shave walking with his girlfriend; he was advertising his stupidity by wearing a necklace dangling bullets. His black leather coat had the slogan "Aim High" on it. Marines? he thought for a moment before correcting himself. No … no. That is the Air Force. The Marines had the one, "The Few, The Proud, The Marines." For some reason O'Connor had to fight off the urge to drive a fist into Dipshit's solar plexus. Stupidity was as evident within this airport horde as toad stools on soggy logs. Then Dipshit spotted him and veered in his direction.

"Sir. Are you military?" The boy leaned into him as if he wanted to breathe the same air.

Well now … Dipshit had balls. No brains. Maybe he'd make a good Marine after all. O'Connor smiled at his private joke. Dipshit looked at him like a kid peering under the Christmas tree.

"No, Baggage Handler. I fly the friendly skies for free, you see." O'Connor made eye contact with him not revealing his true feelings.

"Oh. The haircut. I would've sworn you were in the service. Sorry pal."

There was a reason he had gotten rid of everything military: his uniform, boots, the works. He looked down at his Sketchers and smiled. He'd never wear another pair of combat boots if he could help it. He had his fill of the bullshit buffet and was ready to make life, his life, good again.

Tonya looked up from her book. "You looked military to me too. I was going to ask but didn't want to seem forward. Just a baggage handler. Too bad. You could serve in the Armed Forces," she shivered. "Why after some basic training who knows. You could serve with—honor."

O'Connor stared off into the distance. "I bet you could serve in one of the branches of the service. They take women, you know. Why don't you sign up?"

Tonya lowered her book and spun toward him, face foreword like a person searching for an object gone bad in the refrigerator. She whispered as if she was sharing a state secret. "Well I should really join but I'm thinking they'd never take me. Hypertension, don't you know. I'm on medication. That's why I have to keep food in my tummy." She patted it. "Can't have anything upsetting it."

O'Connor wondered what it would be like to squish an ice cream cone in her face the way guys put out cigarettes. In high school he'd been voted Mr. Manners. He was the kind of guy who got along with everyone. Even teachers. Now here he was thinking about the pleasantness of releasing violence on a fat girl. "Oh that's too bad. Tonya. That's your name isn't it?"

"Why yes. Yes it is."

"Well, I'm just thinking how awesome we would have both been, serving our country. He picked up a newspaper from the floor. Look here: 'Be all you can be. The Army' Tonya."

He was on the last leg of his trip—to a tame place. His hometown. It was a place where folks said nice things for no reason and bad ones got the death penalty for doing what he'd done plenty of.

The flight had been what is referred to as 'uneventful'. Then the park entered his thoughts when he was in the Uber. Maybe he could sort it out there. On his bench. He knew the way. It didn't take long before he stepped on the grass he'd been sure he'd never see again. He wasn't on the walk. He remembered nuns reminding him to stay on the walk to respect those who had given their life for him. It never made any sense to him why anyone in their right mind would die for just a kid they didn't even know. He had to wait until he was war-old and crossed paths with Nicholas before he got it figured out. The grass felt good on this toes peeking out of the cast. He was home.

The American sun O'Connor sat under wasn't nearly as brutal as the Kabul variety. A subtle breeze rattled the leaves. The cement bench had always been there waiting for him. It still had the same chunk out of the arm rest. He smiled and ran his fingers over it. The bench was smack dab in the middle of a bunch of plaques. They all had names on them. Most were from guys who'd died in Lincoln's war.

A grey cannon had been chained to a spot on a slab of cement. It was next to the bench and he patted its cool steel but avoided the darkness of its bore. He had slipped an inquiring third grade finger into it once and got nipped by a bee. Actually, he found out later, it was a wasp. His finger had swollen up to the point where he'd thought it was going to burst. He'd grabbed hold of his wrist and had started following his hand home; the sooner he got to ma, the sooner the finger would settle.

Old Man Fratskee, more clothes than man, had been pushing his mower through thick grass. He had wiry white hair and veins in his arms bigger than the bones. It was the kind of mower didn't have a motor.

O'Connor was keeping an eye on his finger and ran into Fratskee, who took one look and worked the stinger out with a yellow nail. His voice had taken some of the sting out of the finger too. Always a nice man.

They talked some 'bout them damn wasps hidin' in the cannon. He told Fratskee he was fixing to kill the wasps for puttin' the hurt on him. Fratskee told him it wasn't a kind thing to kill for the sake of killin'. Them bees was just defending what it was, what made up their world. They had a queen wasp and babies to keep fingers away from. Fratskee also told him bees make plants grown. They feed birds and some of 'em even make honey. Every life contributes something, is what Fratskee said.

Red, white and blue petunias bordered the walk up to the flag pole. Marnee Tesdahl was a Girl Scout. She stood next to him on the Fourth of July when he was still in Cub Scouts. They had marched in the parade which always started, every year, at Holden's Variety. Really old guys, in uniforms, waited to shoot guns in the park. They did it to help folks to remember dead soldiers.

O'Connor shook his head and smiled. He looked at the exact spot where he stood and asked Marnee why noise improved memories. She told him he was really stupid. Everyone knew Cub Scouts were supposed to be smarter than Girl Scouts if they ever wanted to be Boy Scouts. He wanted to be a Boy Scout so he shut up.

The class project: was that Marnee? No … it was her friend, but what the hell was her name? He struggled and then it came to him. It was … Lucia. 'Luscious Lucia.' All the boys hated him that day he got to go to the park with her.

His eyes followed the pole up to Old Glory. It hung in the still air. They had had to write a report about it. O'Connor's gaze followed the flag pole to the ground where a plaque was bolted into its base. It had names on it from guys in the area.

He didn't have to get up off the bench to read about the war with Germany. O'Connor knew he had some German in him, but he'd never let Lucia know that. He remembered how she had asked if he had kin from Germany while leaning away from him like someone too close to a campfire. That day he had only been Irish though.

He had told her straight away he was gonna grow a pair and kill bad guys and make city folk right proud. At the time it seemed necessary to have Lucia thinking he was a hero. She'd laughed and he'd smiled. Lucia'd told him a woman made the country's flag so Americans knew what guys needed killin'. Bad guys never strayed near the Stars and Stripes. That had been the first time he could recall wanting to kill somebody to be something.

He pulled himself up onto his feet, grabbed for his cane and started for Main Street. Yes, life was good on this side of the world. Be alright with him if he never thought of Wack-a-stan again.

The walk was farther than he remembered. His leg got to achin' and the idea of a beer settled on him. He knew beer and meds didn't mix, but Ma and Pa were still working.

The Cozy Corner pulled him in like a black hole. The place was dead: only three guys playing darts. Music groaned out tunes of cowboys getting screwed over. O'Connor slouched in darkness while the beer warmed his stomach and kept Nicholas at bay.

"Here ya go, friend." The bartender surprised him with another beer. "All day Happy Hour!" He wiped down a table next to him as O'Connor replied, "Thank you." The second beer went down fast and he smiled his way to a third one.

He watched the dart players. The one doing most of the talking ordered another pitcher. He had his cap on backwards with torn up jeans on. His shirt read 'Go in Your Own Jackyard and Back-off'.

The leader of the bunch had a Harley Davison shirt on with a chain going to his wallet. Plenty of muscles did most of his talking. He was burned brown from plenty of outdoor work and dished up one word responses while adding to the conversation. He swirled his beer and looked in it as if it were going to answer an age-old question.

The third guy was skinny enough to disappear if he turned sideways. He was obviously Middle Eastern. He had a white dress shirt on which wasn't tucked in. It hung over expensive jeans. His hair was black as a Montana Raven's.

O'Connor heard the accent and started tapping his knee with the mug. He had no idea which beer the anger arrived with. He drank and listened to the music while the laughing grated his nerves. Why did they laugh so much when little girls with big brown eyes were dying? He seethed and considered the group: one runner, one puncher and a skinny foreigner. Yes, recon was important before one dished up whup-ass.

"Muhammered … are you drinkin' or playin'?"

The laughter drove O'Connor onto his feet as he headed to the bar.

"I am Mohammad … not … hammered."

O'Connor closed in and back-handed the Harley shirt wearer with the mug hard enough to leave a soft, mushy spot where the bones had collapsed in his head. The boy hit the floor hard and

21

didn't move. His second blow, from the mug, found the boy with the stupid shirt on. It was driven into his nose and his face burst like a water balloon filled with ketchup. The boy's hands found his face that contained two confused eyes before he went down. O'Connor kicked him in the ribs for the hell of it. Mohammad was stunned. His mouth fell open. He was next. O'Connor kneed him in the groin and penned him to the floor with his cane pressing down on his throat.

"You want to know why I kicked me some ass, don't you?" O'Connor growled. "Cause you laugh too much. Happy go-lucky little shits. Ain't so funny no more, is it? Just little ol' me and a mug and bingo, you find your manners." O'Connor's eyes had the menace of a snakes. "I ain't gonna mess you up any. Need you to educate your buddies about being inappropriate. Tell 'em one fella don't let me sleep no how. Tell 'em no laughing allowed. A kid died on-purpose. I can't sleep none and I hurt. Tell 'em that."

Mohammad stared with wide eyes while gagging and moving his head up and down under the cane. The bartender had bolted. O'Connor stepped into the sunlight and his world tilted causing him to stumble. Sirens grew louder. A squad skidded to a stop. He heard "Get your hands up!"

A bee landed on him. He swatted at it without thinking. The gunshot wasn't heard but the pain registered. He watched the bee, on its back, move delicate legs. It was dying. It was an accident though. It was the on-purpose kind of killing that hurt most. On-purpose means no laughing. His world swooned before he drove his face into the bee. The blood and squashy jaw bone made it hard to breathe.

Once he started dying the pain dwindled. Nine minutes ticked by. He knew life was the result of an accidental curiosity from the unknown. Time bound all lives together.

He slipped away from time. Being late, or on time, no longer mattered any. He still worried about on-purpose killing and laughing while everybody lost something of value. The voices around him cleared and faded like a distant radio station being tuned in. He had something to say but could only manage chewing motions. Then the girl's eyes confronted him in his darkness. A tear found the blood-puddle under his face. An ambulance crew lifted him onto a stretcher and slid him into the rig in eleven seconds flat. They intended to take him to the hospital; he never made it. He went to the Forever Dark Place—where nobody talks and nobody listens.

The Last Gargoyle

Curt Rude

—Friedrich Nietzsche *"Art is the proper task of life."*

Happiest larks in the meadow are the idiots. Look at one of 'em sometime and tell me I ain't spot on. I know … I know, I'm not supposed to think it, but that don't make it any less truthful. If somebody go and call you a moron how that make you feel? The whole 'created equal' deal didn't take into account the fact some got blessed with big brains and some hardly have the sense God gave a goose. I'm not all bad. I usually don't pick on the less fortunate just because I can. No. I'm all about challenges is all there is to it. I live in a free country and choose to befriend fellas who can maintain their end of a conversation. So I'm the first one to admit I got ugly when a nitwit somehow figured he good enough to befriend me.

I didn't see it coming 'til it was too late. The janitor wiped his nose on my sleeve. Not acceptable in my world. Oh, nobody seen him do it, but they sure heard me. I called him a thing or two. I just so happen to pack a thing called a temper, not that that's an excuse or anything. Boy, let me tell you I felt like I got it all wrong in no time flat. It was like everyone thought I should be kind and understanding and not defend myself at all. Well, I stared down the simpleton, realizing I couldn't hate him anymore even if I tried

24

really hard. He was grinning, but not over anything he'd just did. Grinning seemed to be his preferred manner. The whole thing just bugged me enough to not go to class. I mean I'm not going to sit in class watching snot dry on my sleeve. I got pointed in the direction of my van, but flopped down on the first bench I passed. I sat tight, visualizing the act of vengeance that went from a slap to mowing down nitwits with my van. The pint of vodka came in handy. It helped fuel thoughts of what I'd do to equal the score. Before I got going again, I had decided I would avenge this great wrong. How this was to be done I did not know.

So how in the hell did I become a snot rag in the first place? Everyone parties the night before the first day of classes. We partied, I won a contest and … okay … stayed up all night.

My frat even toasted me with beer bongs. I was the man of the hour and won the 'Hogger Contest'. My brothers called my date a Hog-o-rilla. It was just a 'fun and games' play on words.

We all knew a boar hog could never screw a gorilla and produce my date. I think her name was Sally and she was butt ugly. I got paid the pot because, through no fault of mine, she heard the laughing and comments and stormed off before I could kiss her and collect the cash. So I'm not sure if it was the partying or not, but I couldn't find my art lab. My fraternity is known for being responsible so we all pledged to make it to class either puking or half asleep. So all I want to do is make it to class and sit in the back nursing a severe hangover. My head's pounding and I'm feeling I must look like one of the freshmen loose in the hallway. I ask a custodian, with the name Gary on his shirt, for directions and he wipes his nose on me. How could I know a custodian, named Gary who I hadn't even met before, was my sworn enemy?

After that unforgettable first encounter it seemed like I was always bumping into Gary. He made like he'd gained a friend while I obsessed with evening the score; how does one live with the fact an ignoramus got the better of him? Right?

Gary morphed into a big pain in the ass. I mean the tard couldn't leave me be. Last thing on my mind would be good old Gary and then he'd get to following me around telling everyone we were buddies. I wasn't sure if I was embarrassed or pissed, but the heat would roll off my forehead. There was no shaking Gary so the best I could do is hide behind a wall of laughter. Problem was, the more I laughed the more I hated myself. I knew I was nothing but a limp dick. News would be on in the cafeteria and I'd watch it while downing a sub sandwich. Seemed like every day there'd be a story about a shooting somewhere; left me wondering why Gary couldn't be on the wrong end of a gun. Put him out of his misery and help me some with my state of mind. If I didn't have vodka, I'm serious here, I'd've never made it.

My mother had got the notion that I drank too much. Getting kicked out of my father's Ivy League school didn't help. That's how I ended up in a public school. Sometimes things just don't work out as planned. School struck me as a good excuse to party an extra four or five years. Wasn't long before I was put on academic probation. One thing led to another, and before I knew it, I was in a new school pursuing art. If an elephant could paint so could I. Not a lot of homework to mess with your vodka dreams if you're enrolled in an art program. So anyway … mother made me promise the usual no vodka deal. I care about the feelings of others, so I would go out of my way to purchase my bottles in three separate stores. That way I avoided the look, and I always used cash. If mother asked, I always said something like I needed art supplies. The booze itself wasn't a problem at all. I used the big bottles to refill my pint which disappeared into my pocket. I needed my pint like an asthma sufferer depends on his inhaler.

I woke up on Saturday which meant exercise. A walk to the liquor store. I didn't see him until we literally bumped into each other. I had him in my speech class and he wasted little time telling me all about a problem. He needed cash for gas, to see his girl, and begged me to purchase his pistol. I'm like, "What do I need a gun for?" and he's offering to throw in a box of bullets. So, I end up with a stub nosed thirty-eight. At first, I didn't think I could ever kill anything for real, but that didn't stop me from thinking about it. It was like knowing I was big and bad and nobody best not mess with me. I now had the feeling others in my world were alive just because I had decided they should be. It got to the point where I wished I had always owned a gun.

Monday happened way too soon like it always seemed to do. Time for class and I'm running around with a toothbrush in my mouth wondering how the weekend had disappeared. I find a parking spot and veer to the nearest bathroom on my way to class. Got to do a watercolor picture so I make an exception and lock myself in a stall and take a couple of long pulls on my pint. I usually wait until noon for my medicine but, I got to rattle the shaking out of my hands if I'm going to nail the watercolor. The hands got to shaking after only a couple of weeks in class. Doesn't take an Einstein to figure out it's all about the gallons of coffee a guy has to pound to make it at the collegiate level. Anyways, I'm leaving the bathroom and spot Gary. He stands out like a topless woman in church in his goofy overalls. He's bent forward, grinning and trotting toward me pulling his bangs out of his face. If I had known this, I would have pounded more liquid courage, but hey, I fake a smile. Someone is laughing and I wonder if it's because I am friends with Gary. Today comes with a mechanism of escape. I am late for class. We greet each other and leave it at that.

All's good in class and I nail it. Not sure what came first … the vodka or the Masters, but you name it … Rembrandt or any of the others could have painted better if they were half in the bag. The instructor was radiant and full of praise. She actually leaned into me enough to cause me to hold my breath. Some people come with real sensitive sniffers. Vodka was supposed to be odorless. My mother put any bloodhound to shame with her ability to smell a drop of vodka a mile away. So, I'm down for a ton of praise before the instructor is replaced by one of my frat brothers.

"Dude, no worries in this class. I'm still hanging from last night and can't hold a brush but look at you. All's good."

"No worries."

The praise started getting uncomfortable. Besides I wanted to toast my performance with a sip of vodka. "If I don't see you in the future … I'll see ya in the pasture," and I make for the bathroom like I gotta piss bigtime. After a delicious gulp or two I head to the cafeteria. Stale subs were their specialty. I looked around before ditching into a dark booth to do my first food of the day.

The thought of vodka helping the sandwich down entered my thoughts. I glance around to see if the coast is clear and see him headed my way. Ahh Shit! No escape. Gary wiggled and pushed his way into the booth. I didn't lift a finger to help him, hoping the idiot would dump his tray. Gary was outfitted in bib-overalls—complete with pencils in the chest pockets—and combat boots. The overalls barely touched the top of his boots. He topped the ensemble off with a bright white Stetson. It was like a marquee drawing everyone's attention to the fact I was having lunch with a ding-a-ling. Gary tore open his lunch before working a dirty finger under the bun. He swept mayo out and stared at it.

I leaned back and watched Gary amuse himself with his mayo'd-up finger. He held it over the table, zooming it around like an airplane. The thought of slapping some sense into the clown tantalized me, but it was wishful thinking; kicking bulls in the nuts or messing with Gary's mayo both would end up causing higher life insurance premiums. What Gary lacked in brains he made up for with a shit ton of muscle.

There was a rhythm to campus life. Certain students showed up at certain times. You could count on seeing so and so at such and such a place and time. I was looking for the girl, the so fine denim princess. When she finally stepped into my line of site I totally stiffened. She was one badass lady I'd love to do, but then a loud

30

pop broke the spell. I was pissed. Gary made another popping sound by pushing on the inside of his cheek with his finger and then pulling it out. Just keep it quiet dude—I'm thinking. She must've heard it because she glanced at us. My face felt like a radiator when our eyes met. All's good if I could man up and plant a bullet in his head. I stared hard at a spot between Gary's eyes. He'd taken to smearing mayonnaise around his paper plate with his finger. "Never seen anyone get after old mayonnaise like you, Gary."

"Awe shuck, it just good is what I know. Wanna know sumpting?" Gary's eyes widened.

"Oh Christ here we go—" I figured.

"Sometime ma ain't round I put a big spoon right in mayo jar. I do. She say sumten like 'Where hell is mayo?' after she done work." He looked around smiling like he was expecting a standing ovation.

"Well now … we know the secret of happiness: one bigass dollop of mayo for you and the rest is history. Christ, normal fellas can't figure out happiness," Jonah cleared his throat. "Got anymore humdingers—Gary?"

"You give that girlie-girl 'a wanna see you buck neckud' look."

"What girl?" I dared him with an awful stare. "I wasn't checking nothing out, pal."

"You checkin' her bidness out." Gary pointed. "She givin' you a hard-a-saurus. Uncle Jimbo, he done tell me, gawken eyes pop right out you not careful. Jimbo know it all! He showed the cement thing to me."

"Godamnit Gary ... really. Serious here. Shut it. Please."

Gary lowered his voice. "I figger I knows a thing even if'n I a dimwit."

"Let's cut the shit pal. All's good. Right?"

"I hear stuff pushin' on the ol' broom. Peoples don't see nincompoop custodians even if they holdin' on a big broom." Gary lost interest in the last dollop of mayonnaise on the wrapper. "My ma done tole me it is like that—"

This was the most I heard him say so I'm like ... "I'll be screwed, blued and tattooed. So you know how to listen—"

"I good listener, and you'ze mean as a bitin' sow pig."

"Hi ya. How's my favorite sculptor this afternoon?" The denim princess smiled and patted Gary on the shoulder. His mean eyes disappeared and the stupid grin reappeared. "I can't wait. Are

32

you done with it already? The wait is like totally killing me. Professor Walters is just going to love it. It's for her retirement. I told you that, right? The whole class is pitching in. Oh how much I owe you?" She smiled down on Gary and tilted her head back and crossed her arms. "Oh God, I'm like totally running off at the mouth." She shrugged her shoulders. "Sorry."

"I do work and ma'll do the figurin'. That how it done. I know … then you know. I do good. You good to Gary. So I do real good," Gary pointed across the table. "Him mean an wanna have six with you but no-no to that." Gary stopped talking and resumed his attack on the mayo left on his plate. "I have good stuff. It cost more dollars … white cement … but it holds the paint good."

She shook her head. "Oh God, you're totally amazing. I can't wait to see it. Totally owe you Gary."

"Ma done say I nothin' but a servant. Doc tol' her I good an stupid but best—ah—when a gargoyle a need makin'."

I couldn't make heads or tails out of what was happening. Gary wasn't just a simpleton. Gary made shit with cement a certain chick loves. He was a bigtime idiot savant, which means, whatever he makes must be amazing. And finally, he knew—her. Then he tells her I want to screw her. Good ol' Gary was headed for a dirt nap and didn't even know it. The gun would shut his ass up but good. Shoot and shovel. The hole had to be plenty deep. Yes, I ain't a weak tit no more: I'm'a real stud. Thinking he could pull a trigger and finish off a problem like they do in the movies or in video games released him from what he was: an art student in a two bit university leading to Loserville.

"Well you're the best. They don't call you Gargoyle Gary for nothing. And thank you. What's your name?" her glance pulled him from his gun thoughts.

Gary looked up, "That Jonah. He got a hard-a—"

"Name's Jonah. How are you? Nice to meet you. I'll help get the gargoyle thing-a-ma-jig to you." I had to talk fast and loud. By now I knew Savants damn sure didn't seem to come with any kind of filters. If they think it, they say it. If he opened his mouth again I'd talk over him. No sense in my being embarrassed at the hands of ignorance. People just aren't supposed to say things Gary did. Shoot … Shovel … Shut-up. That's how murder works.

"Off to class and thank you guys." She spun toward the exit and I did not take one little tiny peek. Instead, I turned and looked at Gary's blank face and inhaled. Questions. Where should I start? My jaws were clenched shut so hard they hurt. What did feel good was the thought I was something I wasn't: a killer.

34

"Wow. You know her. You make statues. You make statues for her. Ya got a nickname. I mean holy shit, Gargoyle Gary. You … the … man. Look. You listening to me? You weren't really gonna tell her I had a …" I looked at the paste stuck between Gary's teeth from a lifetime of no brushing. Just as well be explaining physics to a pooch. I twisted a kink out of my back from setting so long. "Cement. How about that? Sounds like you kick-it makin' them-there gargoyles. Right? Who would've thunk it?"

Gary became rigid in the booth. "I got me a Yardmax point six cubic footer to mix contractor grade concrete. It come in sixty pound bags fur sure. I do two bags at time." He held up two fingers. "Bag'll run me thirteen an forty seven cents, plus tax. Good stuff. Set up fast. Gotta weld rebar to make gargoyle stand nice and keep the mean inside, I do. I start at the bottom and pour buckets until the mold is full. Then I tap on it with a rubber mallet to get bubbles out. Then it get dry and stay mean forever." Gary leaned over the table with a smug look, "I got me glass molds, mista. Fiberglass. They cost a ton more than everting else." Gary took a quick breath. "This time 'round I'ma gonna tap in nails to anchor screen over wings. Betta take my time so they don't fall down. That happen I get mad. That called stucco. I got it figgered if ya help me. You help ah me make it good and mean?"

I couldn't believe how spot on and unstupid Gary sounded when yapping about cement. I cleared my throat and leaned toward Gary. "Oh I'll help you alright. We can get it to her in no time flat."

He needed his vodka all of a sudden worse than a babe needs formula. He felt a pint was just what the doctor ordered. If he didn't have booze he wouldn't be able to spend another second with Gary. He was going to do it for one reason, Gargoyle Gary made her— happen.

By the time he got to the van his buzz had worn thin and was replaced with a dull thud right between his eyes. He crawled into the van and sipped his medicine. He always inhaled before drinking the vodka so he could exhale the heat away. He wondered if she thought he was a big enough loser who actually hung out with the likes of Gary. That caused him to take a big gulp he choked on some. He slid the bottle back under the seat and it clanked against the pistol. Then he remembered the tiny bottles of McGillicuddy. They had been giving out free samples. He took a deep breath and hopped out of the van and dashed to the lecture. It had started to drizzle.

The two hour lecture felt like four. He sat by the door just in case a bathroom break for a drink was needed. He marshalled his thoughts. It would all be worth it if he got on a first name basis with her. All good things come to those who put up with the likes of

36

Gary, or at least he told himself that. Then the lecture ended and he was sprinting in a steady cold rain toward the van. He spotted the dark hulk hunched over by the passenger side door. "Holy shit, Gary! You here long? Christ, let's get in the van before you catch pneumonia and die," Jonah smiled, "Jesus you're drenched." Shoot … Shovel … Shut-up.

"Janine want her a gargoyle. Thank you, Jonah, to help me. I know Janine and don't need you to hurt her." Gary, grinning, turned toward Jonah with pain in his eye. "Worse sound on this here plain-nut we live on is a heart breakin' ma say when Sally Mae got dead."

"Christ I ain't a gonna do Janine none."

I noticed Gary was plenty wet. Probably an hour or so standing in the cold rain. Gary, grinning said the gargoyle could be done tonight. I started the van and turned on the heat. "I have just what the doctor ordered for you, Gary. Time for some fruit. You gotta have a serving of fruit every day. I'm thinking apple pie. You want some apple pie, Gary?"

"Oh apple pie. I want me some. Yeah. Gargoyle Gary like the pie with mayo!"

I reached under the seat and felt the pistol before finding the bottles of apple pie flavored Doctor McGillicuddy. "Yes, just what the doctor ordered. It'll warm ya up. An apple a day keep the doctor away." I tossed a bottle down to show him how it's done. Then I relaxed for a spell with my eyes shut breathing through my teeth. "Here. Down it. It'll cure what ails ya. Kills the worms." I like hold a little bottle toward Gary. It's hard to do when you're as thirsty as I am. Right?

"No fruit. Liquor. Liquor. Bad liquor. Drive don't drink or die. No liquor." Gary started pounding on the dash swaying back and forth. "No pie. No fruit. No-no-no."

"Chill. Christ; just trying to be friendly here. 'Never kick a gift horse in the balls,' I always say." So I get to thinking the hell with it and down the bottle. "You okay, pal? Do we need to talk or something?"

Gary stared straight ahead and didn't respond. The van spun out of the lot, kicking up stones. Long day and now I got to put up with more shit. Well screw it. I'll kill another bottle if I have to. He glanced toward Gary. Nothing but shit for brains and he's in my van. Die drinking McGillicuddy. Whatever.

They both heard a bird hit the windshield.

"Stop. Stop. Now!" Gary howled.

"What? Shit. Now what? Jesus Christ. What's got into you? You wanna walk in this?" Gary pushed his door open and lunged out of the van. He pulled the windshield wiper off the glass freeing the limp swallow. A delicate feather swirled away in the rain. Tears welled up in Gary's eyes. Then he started CPR. He blew just a touch of air into the beak and pushed on the breast with a finger. "Call right this minute. You call," he hollered toward me.

I'm totally lost. "Gary. Who do I call? What are we doing here?" I'm like holding my palms up. "I don't get it."

"Ambulance. EMT's. Call. Hurry." Then I watch him carefully breath into the lifeless bird. His shoulders heaved.

"Ahh shit, Gary, that bird's dead. Sorry, but Jesus Christ."

"I don't want bird dead."

"Don't matter, friend, what you want. You can blow on that," I nod toward the bird in Gary's palm, "but it ain't gonna change a thing. Dead is dead."

"Then we go to the funeral home. Now." Gary wiped his face with a drenched sleeve. "Sally Mae went there while God done make a place for her in heaven." His head dropped and he sobbed.

I'm thinking like who is Sally but hey I ain't all bad. I crawl out of the van and tap Gary with the last bottle of McGillicuddy. "You sure you don't want a nip. Might help is all I'm saying with this Sally the swallow thing we got going on here."

"No liquor. No drive. Ma say drinkin' on a half brain leave ya no brain."

I put the van in drive and Gary pointed down the road. I drove on pavement some miles before Gary had me turn onto gravel. Gary was thinking about if the swallow had family that was going to miss him. Leafless limbs hung over the road like old lady fingers tugging them toward their fate.

"Hey, Gary, we almost there? We can bury the bird then make that gargoyle for Janine. That the plan?"

"Yes, that the plan, you mean ol' Jonah. Meaner you is the better."

Gary pointed and finally told me we were there. I was totally creeped out some and pulled into the drive. The barn was long gone, but the silo looked like it was built yesterday. Not a crack in it. The house needed paint, and for some reason, it seemed like all the trees had died around the place. Gary lunged out of the van with his bird and walked toward a pole shed near the silo. I figured he was in a hurry to bury his damn swallow so I dug under the seat for my precious cargo. This business might just require drinking from the fifth. I worked my arm clear up to the elbow feeling around for the flat bottle. Gary pulled my door open and I saw a swinging motion before my world went dark.

When I opened my eyes, the back of my head hurt bigtime. I wanted to feel my head but my arms wear tied to a cage-like-thing I was in. I couldn't move my legs either. Then it all came back to me. The dead bird … and making the gargoyle … and the idiot. Where in the hell was the idiot? I heard the steady hum of a cement mixer, but something else caught my attention. It was sobbing. Serious sobbing. I looked around until I spotted him. Gary was tearing open bags of cement and lining them up next to the mixer. The cage I was in was made of rebar that is used to reinforce concrete. It all came to me in an instant. I screamed! I couldn't move. The cage was inescapable. Two pieces of molding were propped up near my enclosure.

"Gary. Gary. C'mon, man I don't mean to toss any shade here, but tell me this ain't happening. Bill. Is this some kind of joke?" Good ol' Bill was our very own frat jokester. This was just him being funny. I laughed insanely. The pole barn reeked of oil and I noticed a bunch of Gargoyles glaring at me. Oh god this ain't a joke. "Hello, Gary … we need to talk, my friend." My heart raced while sweat dribbled into my eye stinging it shut.

Gary stopped his sobbing. He went to the mixture and dumped cement from it into the wheelbarrow. "This easier if'en you'd stay sleepin' … you wan' another clunk on yo head?"

"Okay I get it. We've just had a misunderstanding. How do I help you if I'm in this thing? I feel like a parakeet or something here." I laughed. "Jonah wants a cracker." Then I force laughed until I looked into Gary's sad eyes. "Oh totally sorry. Why ya bumming, dude?"

Gary picked up one of the pieces of the mold and leaned it against the rebar basket. "Bye-bye Jonah. You bad and make gargoyle real-real bad. Janine gonna like this here gargoyle best because you in it makin' it mean." He made a deep growling sound. He then snatched up the other half of the form and bolted them together, making my world black.

"Oh I get it. Yup … misunderstanding. I didn't kill the bird. Accident. The drinking and driving thing was bad. I gotta make it better. I see treatment coming my way thanks to you, Gary. Please, it's dark in here. Can you take them things down so we can talk this out? I know one thing … you're too good a guy to hurt me."

"I jus' a big dummy, but you say Sally Mae got a boar hog for a pa and a gorilla ma. Ain't so, I'm 'nothin' but stupid but she my sista." His sobbing started overwhelming Gary. "You laughin' and Sally Mae is all time cryin' an' carrying on. She come home but I dumb all time. Don't know nothin' to make it stop. No peoples … not ones wiff a brain or dummies gots no brain should make cryin' happen. Not never on account girls are a lady and sumptime a sista or ma or granma or auntie or sumen like that. I a big dumb-dumb, but know I never do wanna make a girl-person to cry and carry on." His sobs got louder. He pointed his shovel in Jonah's direction. "Sally Mae, she got down in the dumps bad an went an used a belt. Now she gone in a hole and it cold some down there … and I'm all the time sad cause she gone on account of mean ol' you."

Gary paced himself, mixing cement then dumping it into the wheelbarrow. As he shoveled it into the mold, he heard words like "Please!" and "Never again!" He looked down into the mold and noticed the wet mud moving some and hoped Jonah would blow all the air out. That would save him from patching up the finished gargoyle. It wasn't more than a minute or two before everything settled and the concrete moved no more.

One Virus ... One Gift

Curt Rude

—Hippocrates *"A wise man should consider that health is the greatest of human blessings, and learn how by his own thought to derive benefit from his illness."*

"Ah ... Cortez ... there, there. You see it?" She was pointing and sloshed some coffee on her wrist. "Dammit that's hot." She looked down at the liquid dribbling onto the floor.

He looked out the sliding glass door nodding yes. It was the first robin of the spring! Patches of snow littered places the sun couldn't reach. It was drizzling and cold as the bird scooted from one place on the lawn to another. It would cock its head listening for whatever sound the earthworm makes. Then, after detecting no breakfast, it would race across the grass again. Watching robins was just one of many rituals their lives embraced. They both remembered that first walk, holding hands and seeing them, a whole flock of Robins the morning of their wedding.

"Spring is on the way. I love it." Marguerite gazed at the robin enjoying the respite it provided from the virus. She had given up on the news because it left her choking back an avalanche of fears and helplessness. Red body bags never happened in New York City, but then there they were on the six o'clock news. The

44

buildings reaching for the sky in the usual places on the horizon had provided a degree of urban confidence she never knew she had, not until it had been replaced with a feeling that made it impossible to smile. Hating something wasn't in her makeup but she hated it just the same: the coronavirus.

"I love it when the trees turn colors but this is even better." She faced him and put her arms around his waist. "The crocuses should be up by now. The birds are singing in the morning. Thank you for sharing my life."

"Thank you for putting up with a messy old grass cutter." A vague fear, born of an insecurity, lingered; and he thought of the time he first saw her. Then before he knew it, things went from them always being together to him being a dad. That's how their life was changing, just going by faster and faster. He got the feeling they might be in a graveyard before they knew it. One minute his girls were getting Holy Communion, and the next they were graduating from college.

Marguerite had signed them up for senior citizen discounts. At first Cortez wanted to pay the full price and banish the old age thing, but he had come around. Cortez snuck a glance at her and thanked God in his mind. Once when their babies were little Marguerite had to be treated for some kind of cancer. When she got better Cortez had dropped a twenty in the collection basket so God would know how grateful he was.

"We've had a good life. You and me—"

"Don't. Not now. Don't talk like that." As his head kind of ached, he wondered if he had it, if he had it and had given it to her. The virus started as a cough, he coughed while brushing his teeth. Then the headache. His head had throbbed as he'd rub his temple. He'd been sure he'd had it before realizing all he had was a nerve-wracking headache. No need to worry. He wasn't feverish, but he was actually chilled. His thoughts raced around his head, about like sheep getting chased in a pasture by an energetic dog.

"Oh look at the time. The school nurse is going to go over this coronavirus with us. They're nipping the rumor mill in the bud. That's what Caroline said anyways. I can't be late. Wouldn't look good, would it? Darcy works on the ambulance and said they haven't had a call on it yet, so I'm not worried." Cortez was looking at her and knew she was lying.

"You want something to eat?"

"Yes … no. I don't know. If you're have'in something. Just make me something you're having," she hollered, shooting him a glance from over her shoulder as she disappeared down the hallway.

It had worked out well: he made the big bucks while she brought home the benefits, although the policy came with a big deductible.

Outside of her cancer scare they had both managed to stay healthy. Now all they had to do was to be smart and dodge the COVID-19 bug. They'd booked a cruise for the autumn figuring the virus would be gone. A week on a cruise, with a great room, was going for next to nothing. They'd talked about it and both agreed. What a way to celebrate thirty-three years of marriage.

"What are you making to eat? Are you with me, Cortez? I'm in a hurry here."

The question snapped him out of his reverie. "An egg sandwich for ya." He opened the refrigerator. "You can eat it on the way."

"Well, get a move on. I'm running behind here."

It wasn't long before she was out the door and the energized atmosphere evaporated. He took a bite of his sandwich and realized he'd given her the one with horseradish on it. He smiled, thinking about how it would look when she bit into it; she'd think he did it on purpose. A good marriage involved fun and games and both enjoyed them. They might not have a brand new car or stocks and bonds but they did have each other. That was enough as far as he was concerned.

He was scheduled to thatch a yard and do some raking today. The job involved over five or six difficult acres: hills and lots of flower beds and what not to work around. The place was at the end of a turn-around. Cortez called it that but the guard at the gate referred to it as a cul-de-sac. The guard, Steven, always greeted him slowly in a deep voice. "State your name, please. Is Mister Nevis expecting you today?" Although Cortez had been there working many times, the routine never changed. Then he'd look at his license and ask him to state his date of birth. Steven told Cortez a couple of times that "his kind" looked alike so a guard had to be careful. Cortez remembered actually stiffening up, rising off the truck's seat. He had almost asked Steven if he meant all business owners looked the same but didn't. The job paid well enough for him to accept insults; that was all there was to it. His mom, a nurse, told him how to handle name calling a long time ago: "Inoculate yourself against contagious words."

Cortez turned the radio up while making the turn onto Ponce de Leon lane. An announcer had cut in on one of his favorite songs to announce the building of a tent city in Central Park. More people were getting sick. The mayor was working with the state on a response procedure for what was called a health crisis.

He was catching most of the words that poured out of the radio. Words like social distancing, respirators, elbow coughing, pan-flu. He turned off the radio as he pulled up to Steven, dug his license out and recited his date of birth without being asked. He wanted to get done early to be with Marguerite. When his world got too upsetting, her voice worked on him like a hundred pounds of ibuprophen.

Steven handed his license back. "Are we in a hurry today? Please take care to drive in a safe manner while on the property."

Cortez looked up at him and exhaled. He thought about telling Steven what he thought of him, but he knew it was never smart to try and out piss a skunk. "Oh I will certainly do that, Steven, and many thanks for the reminder."

As the chain caught, the gate started jerking open. After driving past the gate he always got a creeping sensation, probably like what a burglar might feel, that it was wrong to be where he was. He wondered if the manicured bushes and magnificent trees would sneer at him if they could. He was a little nothing in a place of huge somethings. As he drove past statues and fountains, his feelings intensified. It reminded him of being in the woods picking up the faint odor of death; if you continued as the odor intensified you'd end up standing next to a maggot-infested deer carcass. In reality he ended up facing incomprehensible wealth which was just as offensive to him.

Cortez pulled up along the utility building where he always parked. Mister Nevis, as usual, didn't appear to be around.

Cortez forgot how he knew, but he had found out Mister Nevis was an investment banker. The only thing Cortez knew about banking was they charged a lot for a home mortgage.

He pulled some ramps out of his pickup before hearing his name called.

"Cortez. Cortez … over here. We need to converse, dear boy." Mister Nevis was stretching his sides from what appeared to have been a long run. He had a sly, feeble grin, on his face. It was a resolute look conveying the knowledge that Mister Nevis had no time to spare.

Cortez hadn't been in Mister Nevis's service for long before he'd figured out the truly wealthy put on airs regarding their ability to converse with those folks who do not meet their assumed standard. He never knew what Mister Nevis thought of him and had given up trying to figure it out. "Yes sir. What is it?" Cortez flashed his on-the-job grin and stared at Mister Nevis's shoes; there was a time to be meek and mild and this moment was, no doubt, just such a moment.

"I simply must pose a rather difficult question." Mister Nevis made like he was putting more effort into stretching as opposed to the discussion. "Let me present it this way. No offense intended—"

"If there is a problem with my work ... not to worry." Cortez leaned toward Mister Nevis. "The motto on my pickup says it all. 'I don't cut corners. I cut grass.' What is it Sir?"

"Are you related ... to any ... of those people?" Mister Nevis's voice quivered as if a dead, bloated dog had explode in his face.

Cortez spun and looked in the direction of the guard shack. He turned back toward Mister Nevis while lowering his voice. "I only know the guy Steven from when I come here. Is there a problem, Sir?"

"No ... no ... not that at all, dear boy. My inquiry is quite simple you see. It relates to whether you have friends or relatives who, how should I say—"

"My son and daughters are college educated. My Marguerite teaches third graders at G-M Public. I went there. So did she."

"Okay, listen up now really close. You have heard of the coronavirus I'm sure. It's going to be a rather, how do I say, unpleasant experience. The governor himself has advised me of a coming mandatory quarantine. I must share something with you that will remain our little secret. The governor's son ran off with a little señorita and now the kid, his son, is sick. He didn't catch the virus out there having fun not practicing safe sex; she gave him a dose of this COVID beast. Perhaps you understand my utter compulsion to pose these rather difficult questions now."

Cortez watched Mister Nevis stretch bending forward to where it looked like his forehead was going to touch the ground. Marguerite had mentioned Cortez needed to be more limber now that he was sixty. He wondered if this was what she meant. If he tried it he'd break in half, he figured. "I have been following it, sir. It makes me nervous."

"Okay then, you simply must understand the importance of our interaction. You see … it is imperative that I have my concerns alleviated. I simply must be reassured that you are not in contact with any of those Wall Jumpers down there in Texas. You know. On the border. I'm sure the border patrol is working diligently around the clock to keep them out, but we both are entirely too smart to even harbor a remote possibility that they catch them all. Then it's the sick ones that'll make it across the border. No offense intended here now. You've been a good—no make that, great—employee in my stead. I am certain you must appreciate the significance of our little get together this morning. I am most pleased our paths have somehow crossed on this fine morning."

"I don't know anyone from Mexico. I grew up here and started my own business. Three of my little ones got to go to college because of my work. Because, like I said, 'I don't cut corners. I cut grass.' That is why I love this country of ours. I served in the Marine Corp, Sir." Cortez used a very respectful tone and waited for the verdict; was Mister Nevis going to fire him?

"Well good then, Cortez. I knew our little Q and A was going to be uncomfortable. Your name … I find a bit disconcerting." Mister Nevis reached out as if to pat Cortez on the shoulder but then froze. "Oh … dear me. One must always be vigilant in these troubling times. It's called 'social distancing'. You should think about wearing a mask anytime you're on my property. And please humor me by using hand sanitizer before entering the premises. I will contact Steven and have him remind you, dear boy." Mister Nevis held out a green bottle of sanitizer and tossed it at Cortez. They both knew times were going to only get tougher so Cortez never considered pulling out of the rich man-poor man game. He just had to put up with Mister Nevis and his insulting questions.

The thatcher started on the first pull, but the noise didn't help Cortez avoid his unpleasant thoughts. He had the impression the world was getting darker and he wasn't sure what was more offensive, a killer virus or rich folks. No amount of thinking would ever answer that question. Rich people had to be smart to have enough money to live like they do. Why couldn't they figure out some Americans didn't have white skin or were named Bob?

The days in New York had grown more ominous with the passage of time. Some who were suddenly working from home had canceled lawn services. Belts were being tightened. Others simply indicated a need to work out some nervous energy. Marguerite was working from home. The deserted streets were not easy on the nerves. Cortez had grown up in the city and found comfort in crowds the same as antelope prefer wandering around in herds. The lion was the antelope's problem; a virus was Cortez's.

Dead is dead and the gift of love had morphed into constant worrying. Was Marguerite okay? How about the kids? Did he even have the right to worry about his own feelings all the time? He finished up the yard work and left for home.

"I'm going to straighten up the shop. Can I get you anything, Marguerite? Peach tea?" She'd always liked Fresca but they were staying out of the market, practicing social distancing, so he'd mixed up a pitcher of tea from powder concentrate after she had drunk her last Fresca. He didn't think it was too bad either.

"Hey, this is pretty good." She held the tea up in the sunlight. "Yeah … who woulda thunk it? This has been in the cupboard since the kids were little."

"Ain't too bad, is it?"

"How you doing, Cortez? … We're gonna be okay. You know that, right?"

Cortez slumped into a chair, cradling his head in his hands with both elbows planted on the table. "Yeah, I know it. We'll get through this." He was quiet for a spell. "I just can't believe hospitals and doctors can't figure out a shot or something. I mean they give us flu shots so why not figure out a cure?"

"Well, think about everything we've learned already."

"Like what?"

"Peach tea from powder is pretty good." She smiled and held her glass out for a refill.

"You must like it. You downed that pretty fast." He carefully refilled her glass.

Marguerite wiped her forehead and took another drink. "Kinda warm in here."

"Yeah, it is a nice day. I think I'll mosey out to the shop now and straighten up some. If this virus ever leaves us alone I'll be plenty busy." After Cortez gave Marguerite a firm hug, like he would never let up, he meandered from the house feeling weighed down, like a cement airplane. He hoped the tools would do something for his heavy heart. There were times it actually hurt like it was going to give out, but once he got his mind off the virus his heart took care of itself.

He no more than opened the door than his phone rang. Does Marguerite need something? He looked at the phone. Mister Nevis. He wasn't scheduled to work on Mister Nevis's Shangri-La estate for just over a week.

"Hello Mister Nevis. May I help you?"

"Yes, dear boy. I am calling to inquire as to the possibility of obtaining your services. I need my place straightened up for a little get-together: pool cleaned, lawn taken care of. You are well versed on the procedure. You will be adequately reimbursed for your effort, dear boy."

"When?"

"Now!" Mister Nevis laughed. "Well, the get together is set for Friday evening. I'll be arriving on Friday around three."

"Yes. I can certainly get right on it."

"Much appreciated, dear boy. You will be handsomely rewarded as I have made mention of already."

It was now Friday and Cortez had been excited all week spending more than enough time getting everything ready at Mister Nevis's place. Steven had even started to flag him through without the usual questions. Cortez had been provided his own key to the residence because the indoor facilitator had actually been struck down with the virus. Cortez had felt like he'd been elevated to a new position in life.

While roaming the residence conducting his duties, he'd done it all, from changing the home filtration devices to cleaning the pool. He looked it over for a final time and was pleased. Everything was as everything should be. Now all he had to do was meet Mister Nevis before the planned get-together that night.

Marguerite watched him back out of the shop. She had developed a dry hacking kind of cough but had put it out of her mind. No reason to jump to conclusions; she had always suffered from hay fever. She figured people still got sick from things beside the coronavirus, but she'd keep an eye on it. Why worry Cortez for nothing? He had worked too hard for this night to have to worry about her. She did feel warm. Was she in trouble? She started getting scared; Lori had told her about someone who got sick and died heading for a test.

Steven waved him through. Mister Nevis was near the service entrance and held a hand up, giving Cortez the feeling of having been selected from the ranks of the know nothings to share a spot on earth with the privileged few. Marguerite would be proud. Who could guess what bumping elbows with the rich and powerful could mean? For all Cortez knew, he could end up accompanying Mister Nevis on his yacht for the next New York Yacht Club get-together somewhere up in Maine.

Mister Nevis had shared a bit of bad news. The facilitator had caught the virus and expired. Cortez was offered additional duties and accepted them without giving it a second thought. He wanted it. Marguerite would want it for them and he could help the kids out.

Mister Nevis had asked that Cortez carry the keys that were left on the lower level of the estate. He was directed to pick them up before leaving for the evening. They parted company, Cortez fetching the keys and Mister Nevis walking off in the general direction of his guests who had started mingling around the white marble pool. The sun had slipped behind the distant buildings of the New York skyline.

The service door was unlocked and Cortez had found the keys right where he'd been told they would be. He put them in his pocket and smiled. It would be a relief he didn't have to ask Mister Nevis where the keys were since he had gotten the feeling Mister Nevis preferred only talking to Cortez privately.

Suddenly he was startled by voices and realized they were coming from a vent.

"It is as it should be. Everyone is dying and we're buying, my dear friend. Just remember, living well is life's best revenge!" Mister Nevis's voice was unmistakable.

"Yes, but this talk of no more dividends. Certainly you've heard of this and limiting share buybacks!" The voice had an English accent.

"Oh … needless worry. Our friends in Washington are bought and paid for. They will see us through this opportunity."

"Spoken like a true gentleman, Nevis."

"That is why I'm on your board, dear friend. We had to deal with the junk bond problem. I tell you, that was a bigger problem than this Kung Flu." Mister Nevis chortled before continuing. "Besides, I see it as a way to cull the crowd. It's just the old and those with preexisting conditions that get nailed by this bug."

"Yes, yes indeed." The English accent was heavy.

Cortez had enough. He jumped in his truck and drove toward the guard shack. Steven spotted him and stepped out hailing him to stop. What now? Cortez thought.

"We have a problem. Mister Nevis would appreciate that vehicle being moved." He pointed toward Marguerite's car.

"She arrived some time ago. She looks sick. I should've called the cops. You're lucky I didn't have her towed. She wanted to see you, but Mister Nevis wants all calls held."

Cortez erupted from his truck and raced to his Marguerite. Her face was flushed and she was sweating. He gently pulled her to the passenger side and got behind the wheel before speeding to the hospital. His heart thumped and tears made it hard to see the road. In her delirium she mumbled, "I love you."

Before leaving the car to find a wheelchair Cortez kissed his Marguerite like he'd kissed her the first time he knew how much he loved her. He sprinted to a wheelchair propped up on a wall near the emergency entrance then pushed it at a dead run back to the car. He kissed her a second time. His love screamed to avenge this unpardonable sin. A man dressed in blues approached the car wearing a face shield.

"Sir, let me help you. Let's get her into the facility. We'll have to conduct tests."

After she disappeared into the hospital Cortez headed back to Mister Nevis's. He parked before turning onto Ponce de Leon lane. Cortez jumped out of the car and walked to his truck. Steven had pulled it to the side of the shack.

"All's good, Cortez?" Steven asked with a faint hint of urban swag in his voice.

Cortez nodded yes. He drove his truck up to the Shangri-La having realized that money scrubs all the decency out of people. His head was pounding and his fever was climbing. He had a gift to share with Mister Nevis and his guests. Cortez unlocked the door and laid down facing the vent hacking and wheezing. He felt horrible. It felt wonderful.

The Trip

Curt Rude

—Oprah *"The greatest discovery of all time is that a person can change his future by merely changing his attitude."*

"Christ, I'm tellin' ya, he's an accident waiting to happen. If I didn't see it coming … we get t-boned. Bigtime! Listen … Babe … if I didn't see the old guff we're toast. That's the long and short of it. You know, once upon a time, it was all 'bout them drunks and druggies scaring the hell out of us. Well … wallah … now they got backup: Old Folks in Escalades."

She looked up from her device. "Who … what Escalade? How do you know he's old?"

Tom repeatedly stabbed his finger in the Escalade's direction. "Right there. That ol' boy would've nailed us good. You listening? If I was still copping, running that red would have been the least of his worries. I don't care if he's … deaf … dumb … and … ancient. I'd write him for careless."

"What's the statute for seatbelts?" She pivoted to face him while raising one eye brow. "Look at you, Tom, operating a motor vehicle without being buckled up. Click it or ticket. Come on, Holmes … Isn't that how it works?"

Amazing. He couldn't believe it. Her sense of timing was impeccable. She did it again: She steered the whole thing in a new direction, from the righteous cop to the law violating citizen. "Look Babe. If they designed belts that didn't hide under seats may be, just maybe, I'd buckle up."

"Well listen up, Mister Sergeant. If you don't buckle up, I shall be forced to make a citizen's arrest."

He took a deep breath and whistled while pulling the belt across his chest. Bridget was right again. He had to hand it to her. A quick glance confirmed her device was sparing him from additional wifey instructions. It was irritating. She could stare at her thing-a-ma-jig and bust him at the same time. Her finger was all over the thing but would slow if something caught her attention: something like Norwegian goulash sprinkled with fish scales, he imagined. He looked out over the stubble of a harvested corn field while a hawk parked on a tree limb. Ah yes, his inner voice screamed—'Free, free … social media ain't got meee.'

He pulled into the passing lane to get around the Escalade. Typical. The eighty-year-old doofus was doing twenty. That's how it works: eighty-year-olds doing twenty and the twenty-year-old's doing eighty. "There you go. He's old enough to have moss growing behind his ears. Told ya so." It was good to be right. She had busted him, but he was back on top of things. He did say the Escalade was being driven by an old duffer. Years of police work could do that: produce perfection.

"You just got to see this." She held up her device and smiled bigtime. "Not now, you're driving. When we stop. Oh, we do have a special family. I love 'em to pieces, don't you?"

He gave her the 'I-heard-you-and-agree' smile.

As the morning sun rose in the sky, it lost its deep orange color and got brighter and smaller. He drove toward it, listening to the thump-thumping of the tires on the road surface. Joints in the cement causing a perfect cadence. He thought he could make it to the next rest stop before he pulled the visor down. He was bored and "visor challenge" gave him something to occupy his mind.

He was also forcing himself to only sip his coffee. He had stopped for gas and asked her if she wanted a cup. She'd told him no and reminded him to only get a small cup. He knew why; they'd be stopping for pee beaks. He was a dutiful husband and only got a small cup. But he was smug in the knowledge he'd scored the high-octane super caffeinated libation. It was good to not be completely whipped. Thirty-four years of marriage did that to some fellas. He had to hand it to her again though. They both could remember when he was a couple years outta college his bladder could hold an entire pot of mud, no problemo. Now he had to hit the bathroom, sometimes if he just got a whiff of the stuff.

He smiled. It was funny now, the time he scooted into a Walmart racing to the restroom. He made it in a nick of time but realized they had torn out the urinals. He figured it had to do with political correctness. Then a young girl stepped out of a stall and froze. He had spun and hot stepped it to the men's room and urinal relief.

"I told you about that time I went in the wrong bathroom."

"Million times."

He started to reach for the visor without thinking but caught himself. Were all marriages marinated in irritation?

"Tell me again if it'd make you feel better." She dropped her device into her purse.

"Nah … I'm good. But ya know—"

"Here we go." She crossed her arms and stared straight ahead, her way of challenging him to pick-up his game. Perhaps that's what thirty-four years of marriage did to a fella: made it imperative that he pick-up his game, keep it interesting, whatever.

"I was thinkin', ya know. Like is this what the getting old deal is all about? Bladders that don't bladder no more. Walking into a room and forgetting what in the hell ya walked in the room for in the first place? Setting glasses down and not finding them for a week? Not using names but saying something like 'old what's-his-name?' I mean my warranty expired. I was at that funeral when that old guy was putting on a show in his walker. He was like older than a hundred-foot oak. It took him forever to get to the front pew in that bigass place. I'm lookin' at him and the urn trying to figure out which one is for me. Is it better to be dead or almost dead?"

"Okay, Lamacker, get to the point. Bladders … now oak trees. Wow."

Lamacker was a wind-bag of a cop he'd worked with in a prior life. He'd never finish a story but just drone on and on. Tom and Bridget had managed to be married long enough to compile words or glances only they knew the meanings of; being referred to as a Lamacker wasn't good.

"Come on. Out with it. Tired bladders. Funerals. Oak trees—" she made a "come here" motion with her left hand.

"All righty then." They both burst out laughing. "I was just thinking is all. You know we're getting kinda old here. Never thought I'd be a grandpa. I remember looking at old people thinking

66

it must suck to be you. Now I'm getting the feeling I'm old. Am I soon gonna start smelling like mothballs? Remember them little shits calling me 'Grandpa Pabst' at Oktoberfest? Just because I did a beer bong. Now it's like if I can't remember the name of the Twins pitcher, it's time to get scared. Alzheimer's sucks."

"Both hands on the wheel please."

They continued driving into the blinding sun. "I can drive with just one hand on the wheel, ya know."

"Look, big guy, we're still young at heart. You're more than a little grey though."

He knew without looking that she was smiling. She always smiled when she pointed out he was committing the mortal sin of getting grey. Hard to deny it when his grandson called a bald eagle a 'grandpappa bird' because it had a white head too.

"Look. I'm being serious here. I'm blonde is how I see it."

"Well, sure then. You're not grey. You're as blonde as Farrah Fawcett in her heyday."

"Whatever. But that's the point: kids now-a-days wouldn't even know who she was. And you know what? There are more and more kids running around with torn up pants and purple hair than there are people our age. The obits are scary. Christ, sometimes three or four of them are younger than me. Man, it's like Diane said … may as well not put off anything for tomorrow, because, well … you know why."

"People still think we're in our fifties."

He looked over at her. "Really, we're like a car that doesn't have any rust or dents. We're cheerful and sprite, but look under the hood and what are you gonna see: an engine on its last leg. No doubt about it. Like that old boy at the funeral. I mean we're all going to be as old as that guy if we live long enough."

"Look … it's the weekend. Can we talk about something else?"

When they made it to a new part of the interstate, the thump-thumping stopped and he'd also won his secret 'visor' mind game. The sun was high enough in the sky to not be a problem any longer and he didn't resort to using the visor.

"Let's see then. What should we talk about?" he said.

"Camping, how about that?" she reached in her purse for her device. "I've bookmarked some places out in Maine we should stay at."

"How about closer to home?"

"Why?"

He couldn't help the smirk that worked itself onto his face. "So ... we can be good grandparents."

"We can do both: Maine and the grand kids."

"You know that was something we didn't screw up." He pursed his lips and slowed down his words. "Our kids turned out good, didn't they?"

"Well, yeah, they did." She dropped her device back in her purse.

"Guess we got lucky is all there is to it. I was a cop and should've known better. I just didn't see it. Jesus-H-Christ."

"What do you mean I should have known what? I'm not following you."

"Oh, you know. Respect your elders. Blah-blah-blah. All that crap. Funny we didn't end up raising a Ted Bundy." He said it while staring straight ahead.

"Teaching your kids to be good citizens is a good thing. Right?"

"Think about it Babe. Priests. Scout leaders. Cops. You know. Authority figures are all elders." He rubbed his eyebrows. "About like tossing a hamster in a cobra pit: Sooner or later something bad happens if you're the hamster; ya can't just hope snakes are nice."

"So okay, this kinda talk irritates me! What are you saying?"

They zipped by several mile markers before he spoke. "Self-preservation, that's what I'm saying here. We should have told our kids to call for a ride if they were drunk. Nope. We pretended they weren't drinkers. They never called but I bet they downed their share. I mean wine coolers aren't sold to wine snobs."

Her voice slowed. "Still not following you."

"Our son, Babe. He served mass. Hell, our daughter served mass but I guess she was safe."

Bridget sat up straight. "What are you saying?"

"No not that. I mean he was not assaulted as far as I know."

"I think I'm getting what you're saying. But we did the best we could. The world was different back then. We didn't know."

He raised his voice. "Honesty is the best policy." He swung his head from side to side while digging at his collar. Beads of sweat had formed on his forehead. "Honest … honesty is nothing but BS."

"What do you mean, Honey?" she asked in an even tone.

"Cop stops a car full of kids on'na Friday night. Cop acts all friendly. Can I look in your car for bombs or guns? He laughs at his joke while being plenty friendly. Driver doesn't know one of the passengers in the back ditched weed under the front seat. Bingo, the driver's busted, the cops happy and life goes on. All the driver had to do was just say no. I mean a cop is not your friend when he stops you. That, my dear, is a fact."

"There was that 'just-say-no-to-drugs' thing back then. Remember that?" She smiled hoping to lighten the mood. "Guess it should've said just say no to cops!"

"Look, we lucked out. We dropped Jane off at Brownies. Christ, talk about hamsters and snakes. Bill's doing time for fondling them little girls. I mean Vicky was a happening Troop Leader. How was she supposed to know she married a molester? She didn't."

"You aren't saying our Jane—"

71

"No. No. NO." He squeezed the steering wheel. "It could've been our Jane, but we got lucky." He cleared his throat. "Don't make it right ... we got lucky and others have to suffer."

He offered her what amounted to coffee grounds in the bottom of his cup. "Oops. Sorry about that. I can hit the next station. Gas is cheaper once we get out of town. You ever notice that? I wonder why that is. Why gas prices are so different."

Bridget ignored the gas question and spoke up. "You were a cop. Cops get cynical. Is that what this is about?"

"You know what it is? Disgust. I'm just not happy with myself. I coulda did better. I coulda been a better dad. I could've stopped playing the game. You know, I just think I could've done a whole lot better. I could have been the change instead of just playin' the game, just getting by."

She looked over at him and didn't say a word.

"I'm not saying some cops aren't messed up in the Think Tank. I mean who wouldn't be a little bonkers watching lawyers defend shit like we dragged into the courtroom. It's bad, Babe, and I don't miss it at all. Man, it'd be a hard one to swallow if one of our daughters was date raped and we had to watch some shit head lawyer prance around in all his legal glory. They all think they are something special. They make the laws and defend shitheads that break their holy rules and laws. And we all know about money and what it does to truth and justice."

"Well ... is it lawyers or bad guys you hate the most?"

"Babe, it's like I hate 'em both. Equal opportunity. You know attorney's prance around and defend prostitutes for cash. I mean it gets confusing here. An attorney will take cash to save your ass and a prostitute will take cash to play with your ass. What's the difference?"

"How'd we get on this subject anyways?" she looked straight ahead. "I'd rather talk about getting old and listen to you bitch about Escalades."

"Well, you can't always get what you want, now can you?" He slowed and pulled into the rest stop.

They sat in the car lost in thoughts. He was proud of himself for not having to hot step it to the urinal. Bridget was hoping law enforcement work didn't do her man in. What he said made her fist ball up tightly. She would have wanted to kill anyone who would do something to one of her kids. And to think ... some horrible lawyer would have been only too happy to get the bad guy out of jail so he could do his nasty deeds all over again. The slamming of the car door snapped her from the grip of conflicted thoughts. She got out of the car and caught up to Tom, almost bumping into kids headed toward the lot.

"You see that kid?"

"Quiet. You don't know how loud you get when you're worked up." She shot a glance back at the kids they'd just passed.

"I mean he's got a ring in his nose: that used to be for bulls and hogs. You know if you put a ring in a hog's snoot they can't root around and wreck fences and stuff? Now we got people wearing them. Christ, go figure. Where's a little peer pressure when you need it? You're a teacher; what do you say to that?"

"They do it for other reasons than to bug you. I mean: green hair, torn up pants, studs in the cheek—it's just how it's done now-a-days. If you were their age, I bet you'd have a ring in your nose."

"If I was their age, I'd want the girl to be prettier than me. I mean these guys are getting their hair streaked and wearing jeans that are going to get 'em in trouble. If they get aroused in them tight jeans something has to give." He started shaking his head back and forth. "I might have ended up with a ring in my nose but it'd been after the fight. What do you do if you have to blow your nose and end up with Kleenex hanging from your shnozz? Good way to put

74

the run on any dates." He pushed the door open and they headed into the building. "I mean come on, Babe. You'd have never went out with me if I had a ring in my nose and three yards of tattoos on two yards of skin."

"Shush now." She put her finger up towards her mouth. "Wait for me here." She broke from his side and headed towards the ladies' room.

Tom felt like it was good to get things off his chest. He sometimes got more worked up than he wished though. It wasn't fair to dredge up every little thing that bugged him. She was the best thing going for him and he knew it. He watched her vanish into the ladies' room and he pushed his door open. He read some scrolling on the wall in front of the urinal. Hard not to; it was only inches from his face. "For goodtime call Lucious Lucia 414-1909." It was actually scratched into the cement board. Determined fella wanted to make sure the message was going to last a spell.

He watched the dribbling effort his body was putting on and recalled those younger days when he could write his name in the snow. Wouldn't be long before his missus would be beating him out to the lobby. Who would've guessed pumps give up the ghost? His dad failed to relate that tiny bit of info.

He stepped out into the sunlight in the lobby and approached the windowed wall. Nice rest stop. The old volunteers, if that's what they were, always lingered around in the closet that doubled as there hide-away office. This one even had music playing. He didn't see the fellow in the office but did notice a large poster behind plexiglass next to the door. It had a very stern-faced black kid, in a sharp Marine uniform, on it. He read the slogan while recalling the one back in his day. It had said something about being one of the few and the proud. Yeah right, he thought. They didn't mention getting blown to bits or being gut shot. Man, it would've been tough sending one of his kids overseas. Just another load of crap he and Bridget had dodged without knowing it.

Someone walked out of the ladies' room but it wasn't Bridget. He spun from the poster to get a drink of water but changed his mind. When he turned back to face the poster, he noticed some words scratched on the plexiglass. Then he thought of Carl and his kid, Jamal. Good kid. Could hurt a catcher's hand with his fastball and good with numbers. Figured to be an engineer if Tom remembered it right. He joined the Marines and almost missed his ride into hostilities because he was answering nature's call. He had ridden into Iraq with his ass hanging out the back of a Humvee; nerves and diarrhea apparently go together. Tom remembered how Carl's voice lowered when he told this story. Because the rest of the story wasn't funny. It was bad and it only got worse.

76

Bridget put a hand on his shoulder causing him to flinch. "Jesus, ya just as well kill a man than scar him to death."

"Sorry. Are you ready?" She turned towards the door.

Tom, still thinking about Carl and his boy, didn't follow her. He stepped closer to the poster and cocked his head to decipher the scribbling. After rereading it, "blk is beutiful-sO is tan-but WHT is the kolor of the big BOSS man" it came to him. Son-of-a-bitch. Some dolt stood where he was now standing. Whoever it was couldn't even spell. Carl and Jamal had suffered too long to have to put up with this. His mind was on overdrive and he was pissed. He wanted to do something but he didn't know what so he kept his mouth shut. He turned and caught up to Bridget who was headed to the car.

"You slammed that door hard enough," she said while he dug for his keys.

They rode in silence for several miles. She asked him if everything was all right and it spilled out of him. Everything about Jamal and the war and how Carl thinks he lost his son in Iraq. Then he explained the poster and the message.

Bridget listened then said, "Jamal is one of my former students. Bags groceries down at Cecile's. He's changed. He was a good kid. Never a problem you know. Now I wonder what his mom thinks when police are in the news beating blacks. Does she worry about Jamal getting in one of his moods with the police?"

"Well, you don't think a cop scratched that into the poster. Do you?"

"No, jeez Honey. I know it's the hate thing going on. Qanon and Proud Boys always in the news. I suppose it's some kid wants to be a big badass white supremacist or something."

"Carl kinda worries some about cops being around Jamal. He's kinda hard to get along with, ya know, when he's chugging the hard stuff. Carl asked me when they gonna get around to legalizing pot. I don't get it, but I guess it mellows Jamal down or something. They told him at the V.A. he could get some for medical reasons, I guess, but they can't afford to be running up to the Cities all the time. Jamal don't like the idea of breaking the law either. Can ya imagine that? He won't score any weed on the street. Not even if it helps him get a good night's sleep."

Bridget was back on her device. "I told you he was a good kid. No, don't get off here, keep going." She pointed down the interstate.

Tom was a bit miffed with the device being out but didn't bring it up. "Aren't we going to Sam's Club?"

"No … I got an idea. We're going to Houghton." She pointed at her device.

They drove in silence until an idea popped up in his mind. "I should've torn that poster down. I could've told the janitor dude or whatever they're called why I was doing it."

"Wow. You went from not wearing your seat belt to crim-damage to property."

"Well Christ, think about it. We've been talking about how we got lucky with our kids. They didn't go to any war and play the killing game: you know, shoot before you're shot. Least I could do is turn around and deal with that poster. I'd feel damn good about it too."

Bridget thought a bit before responding. "Remember when we were in Colorado? Remember when they legalized marijuana there? They had all them sheriffs going on and on about how pot is a slippery slope to heroin. How sex crimes were going to soar. Jails were going to fill up bigtime. Remember?"

"Yeah. Then crime rates went down. I remember. Really chaffed my ass how Wyoming had that check point on I-76 looking for dopers heading out of Colorado."

"Well, Jamal really looks up to you. You coached him on the department's baseball team. He listened to you. Right?"

Tom snapped out of thoughts. "Wait a tick here. Where are we going? What'd you call that place? Haunted?"

"No. Houghton. Houghton Michigan."

"Why would we do that. Are you serious? No tooth brushes. Nothing, and you just want to drive off to Houghton?"

"Remember last fall? We were at Copper Harbor camping. We drove by this … she pointed at her device and smiled. Dispensary. It's called Northern Specialty Health."

"What are you getting at Babe?"

"Don't you get it? It's a cannabis dispensary. They sell weed. We can do this for Jamal. Pick him up weed. Our kids didn't get screwed like he did but we can help. He'll listen to you. About bullshit laws and lyin' lawyers and everything else we talked about. Jamal needs help. You can tell him to take care of himself. He trusts you."

A smile crept across Tom's face. His chest ached with love for the woman he'd married so many sunrises ago. He didn't trust his voice; it could crack. He didn't blink; tears could happen. A certainty presented itself. He had to do it. They had to do it. One act of kindness for the tired, used up, discarded souls lingering on the fringe. One tear worked its way down his cheek before his hand found it.

The Rainbow Flag Allegiance
Curt Rude

Cruel designs reign—until confronted by love.

"Here Kitty-Kitty."

Thankful hobbled from the bedroom to the kitchen table. She had fired up the laptop, while still in bed, to check if Ray Sanders, one of Thankful's school tormentors had died from terminal cancer. Having been given six weeks, she was hoping he was still suffering and not dead; no need to hurry since once the dying thing is over, suffering stops. After a nano second of guilt, old Ray-Ray's constant taunting made the thought of his dying, pleasant. He had loved to tell her she looked like the back of his sack. That kinda thing makes death watches enjoyable. The quick death of Janice, another classmate, troubled Thankful. Any tormentor's quick death was unfair in Thankful's mind. Overweight Janice, at two-eighty, was no lady. She had a mouth on her. She died doing what she loved. Deer hunting. It was reported she had been mistaken for a deer and shot. Moose more like it Thankful thought. But Raymond had suffered plenty cashing in his life insurance policy. Nice!

Kitty Carlisle, a stub-nosed Persian, sprag into her lap.

Ray and Janice's words dredged up horrible memories. Thankful didn't want to have to put up with nightmares, but it was out of her hands. "It had taken everything I had to march into that school, day after day … and … month after month. I swear my heart got to beating hard enough I thought I was hospital bound. Then I couldn't breathe. Felt like one of them critters on TV squeezed by a python. The real me was hiding between a broken heart and humiliated soul. If the tide goes out and land locks a crab, gulls move in for the kill. That's what I amounted to: a clawless crab. Couldn't defend myself worth a damn. "We freshmen," they'd say, "you, 'fresh-for-men.'" I'd a preferred getting caught up in a school of jellyfish," she said shaking her head no.

Thankful scrunched-up her nose and held the cat inches from her face. Kitty Carlisle never got sick of hearing the same old stories. Over and over. Therapeutic is what her cat time was. Thankful rubbed the lone star on the top of the flag she had left on the table the night before. It was deep blue and included a farmer and seaman with a moose resting under a pine tree.

Pa had claimed to be the farmer on the flag: same full beard. She loved their time spent on the banks of the Benjamin Tidal River all them summers ago. He'd tell her stories about pirates sneaking up the Ben to bury treasure. "William Kidd showed up here," he'd say. Then he'd holler, "There he is now!" and tickle her. "The river told me about them pirates and it told me to marry your ma." She never heard a word come out of the river. There was a dead cow or two and a horse in it though. Her grandpa and pa had pushed them in the Ben to disappear with the John Deere 4020. Pa made her promise to stay out of the icky old river. It was full of dead animal sink holes.

"My two problems just grew on me," Thankful told Kitty, "a left and right breast. Flat chested gals with no titties got mean, real nasty, when their prayers were ignored. Not that I prayed for mine now mind you. Then the boys noticing made matters worse. If I could've crawled to an all-alone place, you can bet I would have. That didn't happen. I'd shop with ma and she never did figure out why I nixed every cute blouse or pair of pants she pulled from the shelf. Never wanted nothing cheap or too expensive. No name brands. Stayed away from the L. L. Bean Outlet. Hard to vanish wearing sporting duds.

Funny thing: walking around with a boat load of stress produced a rash, right on my neck. Kids diagnosed it as syphilis. Never mind I was really, really stupid, in all things sex. Virgin with a STD. Go figure."

Kitty purred while Thankful fell quiet and stared out the window. Things were brightening on the horizon. Nothing like a sunrise over the Eggemoggin Reach. Shadows would grow back from sail boats anchored off shore.

"Oh, I know I should forgive and forget but I just can't. Pastor Rodreguiz, God bless his soul, is always carrying on about what Jesus would do. Turn the other cheek," Kitty yawned, looking up at her. "I found out, Miss Kitty ... I believe in no mercy for folks got no mercy. Hard to be decent when you have a bad case of— Nymphomania—after all." Thankful shuttered and rubbed her temples. "They were wrong, Kitty. That's all there is to it. I was never that thing, a nympho, and they knew it. I was unfortunate to have breasts before anybody else. Then I topped it off getting pregnant—and I paid for it."

One more douchebag, Kitty. Dicky-Dick swan dived into a rock. Nice. "Hey everybody ... here comes ... Oh I'm so Thankful for the screwing." Holler that into a girls face and you are guaranteed a pair of dry eyes at your funeral. When he'd seen the pain in her eyes, he'd hollered it a second time for good measure. He had said it right to her face and his eyes kinda had a mean dog-gonna-bite you glint.

It had been a wonderful service for Dicky: stinky roses and plastic organ music. Best thing about it for her was knowing words weren't going to slither over his teeth and out his mouth no more.

He was in a metal casket with a fish pole engraved on it at room temperature.

Thankful settled onto a kitchen chair and thought about her day. She had more time without Brandy around. She did well in school. Good enough in fact to be in the nursing program at Boston College. Had to have a twenty-seven-point eighty-nine percent GPA to get in. One daughter and what a daughter she was. It was hard to believe some thought Brandy was just a mistake an abortion could erase.

Thankful found herself staring at the orange light from the coffee pot glowing in the first morning light. Very quiet today she observed; no waves smashing into the boulder strewn shoreline. Sometimes the ocean would get worked up enough that she could hear the roar from her bed—Mainers called it an Angry Atlantic— and weather reports would mention it. If you make your living in a boat, you need to know what kind of mood the old Atlantic is in.

Thankful used to go to Helen's, a great restaurant, on the Downeast Highway. Prices were good and the food was even better. But she valued adult conversation, more so than the food. They'd discuss things like the price of bellies: not pork bellies, whole belly clams.

They'd also discuss falling lobster prices; the co-ops never paid enough to keep anyone happy. Thankful never cared what the lobsters—known locally as "bugs"—were topping in the market. Made no difference to her if bait and diesel prices at the dock were making it hard on lobstermen. She did care, however, when a classmate once sat next to her at the counter and carried on as if the past had never occurred. He had gotten fat over the years. Perhaps selling insurance will do that to you. She had hated smiling at him while wondering if his pending heart-attack was going to hurt. All she wanted to do was avoid him like cancer. By the time the last sardine cannery left for Canadian shores, Thankful had given up on Helen's.

"I love our mornings together, Miss Carlisle." She scratched the cat behind its ears as the coffee pot got to sputtering and spitting indicating the coffee was ready. She heard the low thumping of the diesel as the boat swung around a lobster buoy putting its attached rope near enough for the sternman to hook. As a boat circles, the rope is looped over a power takeoff. He has to be quick about it. Pull the trap in; empty it; measure the lobster carapace; toss back the small bugs, known as "shorts;" and change the bait bag.

She could tell the lobster boats apart by the cadence they produced running from one trap to the next. This boat she heard was captained by Nolan Connel. He used expensive lime green paint on his buoys with a black cross splayed on the side. Loster boats were music to the ears of the locals.

After spotting his boat and rowing to shore, Nolan would on occasion swing by to check-up on Thankful, his favorite Flag Lady. He was the laughter in her life. Nothing he ever said made complete sense, but then again … that was why she enjoyed him. They had something bigtime in common: he loved Josh near as much as she did.

As she drained her first cup of coffee, she realized Reny's had more coffee brands than Walmart but she'd picked the cheapest one. Now she was going to have to make more trips to the bathroom—not good when you're favoring an injured ankle.

Thankful glanced at her ankle, now swollen to twice its normal size but still not black and blue. She positioned her foot on the floor and applied a little pressure: not good. She could move it though and hoped it wasn't broken. She wondered why cities started putting curbs on the sides of streets. She would have never sprained it without the curb.

Her first challenge of the day was going to be getting out to the flag pole. It had to be done, whether calm seas or high waves. Just another challenge in a life full of them. She shook the flag out with a snap.

"Going to need a new flag," she mumbled. "The wind even tore out one of the grommets. Can't have that. No, Miss Kitty, we can't have that now, can we? This here flag has to fly every day." Nolan had told her flags were just symbols for the "symbol minded." He knew what an upside-down flag meant to her though. She had told him enough times. Soldiers die fighting for flags. Her soldier, Joshua, had died before his time fighting for his tormentors, the very people who had exiled him into the military. This struck her as upside down thinking.

Thankful had first seen the neighborhood twins at five or six years old on tricycles when they had stopped to watch her raise the morning flag. Then, over a decade later, they were supposed to have been playing in the Waterfront Park and Marina Concert. Thankful had arrived before the crowd and gotten confused when she couldn't see Mikaela or Michelle on the stage. She had worked her way to a different vantage point to find the twins when she rolled her ankle. No one but Gloria Birkenstock seemed to have realized what had happened.

It was embarrassing having Gloria Birkenstock fuss over her as Thankful limped to her car. "You just be grateful you ain't got the kidney stones … now that's real pain," Gloria had said. Thankful wasn't listening. She was grimacing. She got help back to her car and managed to hobble into her house, but her swollen ankle made sleep impossible.

She still hadn't gotten word about what had happened to the twins last night as the sun was pulling up off the ocean and birds had begun singing. She leaned forward in her chair as if to shorten the distance to the flag pole.

Then she spotted something she hadn't expected: Brandy's Slug Bug was parked down the street toward Harriett's place. Gloria Birkenstock must've told Brandy about her ankle. Leave it to Brandy to drive all the way home to check on me. Made sense though. Brandy was going to be a nurse after all. "Miss Kitty Carlisle, it appears we have a surprise visitor this morning or did you already know that?" Thankful figured Brandy must have snuck into the house last night.

As a car door slammed, then a second one, Thankful turned to see who was making the racket. It was a deputy and Pastor Jesus Rodriguez. First no twins at the concert. Then Brandy shows up and now this. How many more surprises were in store? she wondered. She felt trapped. They were walking across her front yard and she had not even washed her face, let alone put make-up on.

The deputy stepped up to the screen door while Pastor Jesus stood behind him. The officer, more of a kid than a cop, tried to say something but his throat squeaked. He reddened and shut up.

"Miz Thankful, we are here to discuss Brandy," Pastor Jesus said.

"Brandy?" Thankful said. "Why, she got in late last night from down in Boston. She's going to school to be a nurse. Doing very well—"

Father Jesus cleared his throat. "She left me a message I got this morning. I need to see her. The call … well I shouldn't go into it any more than I have already have, Thankful. These matters are confidential, you understand." Father Jesus stepped past the cop and opened the door. The cop followed him into the living room.

"I don't understand. Lord knows what Harriet Ulland will be thinking: police at my house." Thankful looked toward Harriett's but didn't see her. Thankful cleared her throat and planted her hand on her chest. "Brandy got in late. Do I have to wake her?"

"We just need a word with her and we can be on our way. You understand." The cop said after finding his voice.

Thankful winced as she stood up. The ankle hurt more now than last night, but Brandy will know what to do.

As the cop stepped around Thankful heading for the closed door, the pastor offered to help her back into the chair after noticing her enormous ankle. She heard the cop pounding on the bedroom door before pushing it open.

The belt was looped over the closet door and had cut into her neck. Her pasty eyes were half open but seeing nothing. Brandy's legs were splayed out in different directions like a new born colt. Thankful lost her breath and squeezed her eyes shut, wanting to will it all away. Her ankle was throbbing as she sobbed. She lost herself in the frozen state that comes from having offspring beat a mother to the grave. Then she found her voice; it sounded to her like it was echoing down a tunnel.

"Do something. Breathe. CPR or that yellow shock thing you guys have. Get it! We can't let this happen!" Yet nothing was done because nothing could be done. Brandy was cold to the touch and stiff. Thankful somehow knew this just by looking at her daughter it was over. When the officer cut her down, Thankful felt numb, like a cement statue, frozen in place.

Thankful mumbled but then decided to remain silent. Talking involved energy and she did not have a lot of it. Ma had always pointed out the importance of being hospitable to guests. Brandy had invited them if that's what you'd call it, so, Thankful didn't figure they were her guests. Thankful was confused. She didn't want them in her house, but she felt an acute desire to keep them around. She needed answers but was tired. Crying seemed to be in order but no tears came. Why do cars drive by and someone mow the lawn when my world is on pause?

She was experiencing anger, pain and fear at the same time. Brandy had no right to do this. Who would she do such a thing? Then it occurred to her: Brandy had come home to be near her in her final moment on earth, because dying was a scary proposition. A tear welled up in her eye before cutting a warm path to her chin. Death made no sense; it was so permanent.

Later the morticians arrived. Pastor Jesus had pulled up a chair and was looking down at the floor. As the morticians were pushing the gurney through the kitchen, Pastor Jesus started reciting some words while Thankful petted Brandy's hair, the same hair she had brushed so many times before. It seemed so long ago. "Oh, Brandy ... Oh, Brandy," was all she could say.

Brandy's daddy, Josh, had changed everything for Thankful at "Highschool Miserable." Thankful had been picking up books after someone nailed her with a shoulder causing them to land in a puddle. She had been a nobody while Josh was an everybody: he played football. He drank beer and talked back to teachers. She heard Josh tell the laughing bitches to beat it while Josh helped Thankful retrieve her books. Why couldn't it have been anyone else but Josh? She was steamed lobster red in the face. Josh and his buddy, Nolan, helped scoop her books up and in the school they went. Nobody was talking until after Nolan said something funny or stupid to clear the air, when they all laughed.

Packing rotting alewives into small nylon bags resulted in lobstermen smelling like dead fish. When the raunchy smell found her nose Thankful knew her friend, Nolan Connel, had stopped by. He had slipped into the house and pulled out a chair.

"Nolan … Brandy's gone. I don't know what I'm going to do. She's—"

"I know. I know. I saw 'em when I was comin' in on the Eggemoggin. Tied up right fast. Didn't look good to see the cops around here." Nolan Connel had named his boat the Sandy Brandy. She had Josh's eyes. Best buddy he ever had was Josh. "I feel worse than a racoon spotted by an eagle … out on the tidal basin. Ya can't run and ya damn sure can't fight."

"She was the best thing I had. She was gonna be a nurse. I told her about her daddy and you being war heroes. Now she gone. Now she gone. I don't have no more room in my heart for nobody else. Just Josh and Brandy."

"This world don't make a lick a sense," Nolan murmured. Neither of them moved. They shared a numbed silence. Then he started mouthing words … "'The sailors say Brandy, you're a fine girl; what a good wife you would be.' Thankful, I'd sing that to her over and over again. Yeah, her eyes really could steal a sailor from the sea. Don't know what to do now is all there is to it."

The Ellsworth American was Thankful's news source. Second oldest paper in Maine. She'd first turn to the obits to see who was dirt napping. It was a part of her day more important than food. Now Brandy's picture was going to haunt this page. It wasn't fair. She wanted to know why the world had stopped for her but everybody else could keep living normal lives. She looked at Nolan realizing all the questions coming to her had no answers.

Thankful looked at Nolan. "Josh and I fell in love. Josh was mine. When I began showing, I was labeled a 'nympho;' classmates wouldn't tolerate babies. They were all wrong. I wasn't a nympho."

I went home when Josh left for Basic. I thought the answer was in Pa's gun cabinet. Longest walk I ever made, I tell you. That Remington 870 was heavy. I was crying and could not get the shell in it. Then Bandy kicked me. She saved me, Nolan. Why couldn't I have saved her?"

Nolan shook his head no and held his palms up from the table. "I'm gonna get. You going to be okay?" He rubbed her shoulder before wandering out of the house. "I'll fetch your flag. That ankle still looks a might sore."

Brandy was cremated. The urn was heavy. Thankful looked at it on the kitchen table and didn't know what to do. Pray to it?

She took the top off the urn and slipped two fingers into the grey powder and scooped some out and tasted it. Once upon a time Brandy had been inside her; now she was again. A life without Brandy was meaningless. Now she was gone.

Brandy was still in a stroller back when Thankful went to Reny's for her first flag. The nice cashier boy had asked her if she needed help with the pole. She waved him off. She liked the idea of doing things herself. Nobody figured a lady could do a thing.

The flag idea just happened. When Joshua went to war and never came back, she went right out, got her flag and flew it upside down. Not half-mast. Upside down. So, they'd know. Pa didn't understand the sense in flying a flag upside down but Ma told him to let it be.

The first Wednesday after she lost Brandy, she grabbed her flag and meandered out to the pole. It was pouring rain but she did

96

not notice it. The rain hid the tears. Her mind was focused on getting the flag up in the morning wind. The flag whipped around and slapped her in the face before she secured it to the line. As long as she was doing something, it felt better, so she walked to the mailbox.

A small package from Amazon caught her attention. She'd forgotten what she'd ordered and then picked up the letter. Another bill? No doubt. Then she spotted the handwriting and dropped the package. It was from—her.

Dear World

A monster forced a baby in me and I hurt. I did something that was too easy. Now a baby is gone and I don't know why. Now I'm gone and I know why. Because I'm not strong like you momma. Because I don't want to see people. Because I killed a baby.

Forgive Me

The Ford bumped the curb behind her while she stared at the letter getting soaked in her hand. Nolan jumped out of the pickup and shook Thankful's shoulders. "I'm gonna have to get you rain gear off the boat … you get to doing this. You'll catch one helluva cold." Nolan escorted Thankful back to the house.

As Thankful stared at the wall she mumbled, "How much you hurt before you don't feel it no more? I didn't tell her what she needed to hear. Nobody's perfect. I got pregnant when I was fifteen.

"Her daddy ran off to fight because Muslims weren't as scary as folks in these parts. That dumb old war didn't kill him. People in these parts killed Josh sure as they killed something inside me.

"It was hard back then to be a single momma. I was told that I was nothing but a fifteen-year-old nympho. That's how they made me feel. I was back to being nothing but a dumb slut. Skank. A hoser. They hated love. That was the problem all along."

Nolan looked up at her. "You being too hard on yourself now. You know that, Thankful. I am just plain disgusted with how folks act. They miss the part in church about not judging. They make me ashamed to be human. I do not recall anywhere in the Good Book where hate is recommended."

After chewing her lip she started talking fast—like if she talked slow, she would forget what she was going to say. "I was for sure people in Ellsworth killed Private Joshua. I never ever gave it a second thought. No sir, Nolan. It was friends and family killed him. Pa carrying on how seventeen-year-old Josh was going to jail for statutory rape. Ma crying and getting all worked up on account her very own fifteen-year-old daughter was going to hell. Their friends gave up on my folks. Ma quit the church.

"All Josh wanted … was to do right by me. I wanted to do right by him. We loved each other. Wanting to do something right, together, is love.

"My own pa didn't have a lot of patience around that time. Farming's a hard way to pay the bill. Nobody carried on with Pa the way they used to. He told Joshua boys like him belonged in Shawshank. We never got to hope and dream and be happy. We got dog talked is all."

Nolan did something he never did: he buried his hands in his face and sobbed. "Josh got all full of hate and wanted to get some killing in. Damn. He changed over there. Became a damned good soldier. I wanted to march off with him but Dad had different ideas. Wouldn't let me go with a boy who does things Josh went and did to you. Child Molester is what Dad claimed he was.

"I waited six months. It could've turned out different if I had his back." There was a long pause. "I killed my share over there. More I killed, the less I thought of my dad and what he said. Got bad. I shot an unarmed kid between the shoulder blades, for Christ's sake. I told myself maybe his dad was the one took Joshua from us.

A lot of me never came back from all that killing. Now, no Josh …
No Brandy."

Nolan watched the flag. "You and your upside-down flag."
He rocked his head back and forth. "They're all effin' idiots." He
forced a laugh full of pain. "Sternman will be waiting. Best get after
them bugs. Got three hundred traps to work today."

Thankful watched him get in his pickup and pull away from
the curb. Then it all crashed in on her. Like a tsunami. She crumbled
to the floor. Brandy. Pregnant? Brandy all alone. Rape? Brandy.
Abortion? Grief knocked her down. She couldn't figure anything
out; that part of her brain had shut down for business.

A police report—was there one? Should she look? Then she
remembered the Handcock deputy had done some checking but
hadn't uncovered anything. So how does anyone be so sinister, hurt
a girl, then live with themselves? Why, just glorified animals is what
they are.

She looked over at Kitty Carlisle on the couch. No, animals
would not do it. It takes a human being to be so evil. She got up and
wandered to the kitchen. She knew it was going to be a long day.

Come Thursday she woke up tired. She wondered if she'd
slept at all. She drank coffee as the sun came up. Did she want to put

100

Brandy's ashes into the Benjamin Tidal River? She decided it wouldn't be proper to put her with dead livestock. She looked from Brooklin toward Deer Isle. Brandy had grown up here. She decided she could take her time. She had plenty of that. She picked up the flag without thinking, went outside and went through the motions: pull the line down and the flag up. She had almost raised it right-side up. Distracted bigtime.

"Ma'am."

She spun hard to face the intruder. "Well, you could just as well kill a lady than scare her half to death."

"Oh, ma'am, I'm sorry. I can come back if that's better." The boy, who could've been eighteen but not shaving yet, had dropped his five-gallon bucket containing colored spray paint, brushes, a rag or two, and some blue tape. "Sorry. I'm Dalton from church. Didn't mean to scare you." He was tossing everything back in the bucket. He suffered from being too polite. "I remember that flag clear back to when I was in kindergarten. Why, everyone knows about it. Not everyone flies 'em upside down. I was going to paint. Behind schedule with all the rain."

"You here to paint for me?" Thankful asked.

"Well, kinda ma'am." The boy looked down at the bucket. "I'm here to paint your mail box post. For the Pride Flag project the minister talked about. You must of signed up. I saw your name here somewhere." The boy pulled out a small notebook and ran a finger from name to name.

"Church? Yes, that's right. I signed up. Donated ten dollars. At the bean suppa. Them colors are about respecting people. Yes, I remember now: gay folks, transsexuals, lesbians, bisexuals. Please take all the time you need. I'm so sorry. I'm getting forgetful."

When she got back into her kitchen, she looked in the freezer for her pink lemonade mix. She hoped the boy liked lemonade.

While pouring water from the plastic can over the mix, she heard a ruckus. She looked out the window and spotted a heavy-set guy disappearing down the road while howling at the boy from church about being as queer as a three-dollar bill in a whore house on a Saturday night. The name calling had no purpose other than hurting Dalton. Thankful noticed yellow paint had been dumped on him.

"Oh dear, he dumped paint all over." Thankful motioned toward her garden hose. "We'll get you spiffed up in no time. You might run out of yellow paint though. Most of it is on you. We can use the hose."

Dalton took his Patagonia Coat off. Thankful held the hose and Dalton scrubbed the clotting paint out of his hair and off the coat. She fetched him lemonade and they talked.

"It breaks my heart to hear what that fellow hollered at you. People have no right to mouth off like that. I get so tired of wars, raping and shootings." Thankful said.

"You never get used to homophobic people and their stupidity. I want to paint and get people to think. Really think. I appreciate our church and the message about being gay and respected. The Pride Flag means things like love being love, kindness being everything, and no humans being illegal."

"We all have our cross to bear. I was called a slut in a prior life. Hurts, doesn't it?"

Dalton nodded. "It really hurt the twins. They missed the concert in the park." Dalton peered down the road. "That guy hurt the twins more than he hurt me."

After Thankful heard Dalton repeat what had happened to the twins several times, she decided to do something about it. Not with words but with action. Not because she hated but because she loved.

People come and people go according to their schedules. Some have to get to work, some have to pick kids up at school. Thankful could set her watch to certain cars carrying occupants to their destinations. While she was hanging her flag in the morning, Harriet would be heading twenty-eight miles north to Ellsworth. Both would wave. They were part of each other's lives but would never talk. While pulling her flag up, she would watch the same guy walking north. She would smile and wave. But he would look the other way.

Tonight she was going to be ready when he came hoofing past her house. That gave her the whole day. First brick painting and then she'd have to retrieve the chest from the granary. It was on the small side but otherwise—perfect. She'd load it with the bricks and push it out into the incoming tide, knowing it would sink. It would go down just where she hoped it would.

"Nice!" She said in a determined voice. "My luck is holding up." The climbs up and down the embankment would serve as a perfect cardiovascular workout. No need for the Peloton.

After her plan was in place Thankful treated herself to Momo's Cheesecake for the energy boost. The cheesecake was double chocolate, and if it didn't power her up nothing would. Her thoughts involved a project that had to succeed. Sitting still wasn't an option. Thankful felt like she was on an Easter Egg hunt again around the farm. She could not miss him because waiting another day was impossible. There were plenty of weeds in the front yard to keep her busy and she started pulling them from around the flag pole.

Just when she was ready to give up, she spotted him, wide as he was tall and slouched forward. He was thumping along on her side of the road but crossed the street. She stood by the mailbox, timing it perfect. She opened the box and looked up as if surprised. The tide was out and the bait was visible.

"Hello sir," she smiled. "A word?"

He shot her a glance but kept walking.

"A word … can I have a word with you?"

"Yeah okay. If it's on account of the other day he had it coming. People like that, queers is what they is, they awful. It says so right in the bible. That's the worst kind of sinner … a mortal … sinner. God'll make 'em into salt. That in the bible. Buttercup and Fruit Loop is what everybody calls 'em: that fella, Dalton and his boyfriend."

Thankful played along. "They'd be picked on plenty back when I went to school. Oh dear. I know that for sure. I can just imagine what my classmates would have told them. Stuff like they being a little light in the loafers. Now enough of that. That is beside the point. Listen to me now. You ever hear about Captain Kidd? You know … the pi-rate?" She strung out the word—pirate—for his benefit. She knew the bait had to be displayed and then the hook set.

"Who hasn't? Pirate sailing around here hiding treasure." He swung his arm around toward Eggemoggin Reach. "It's all bullshit. That Oak Island business about Kidd's lost treasure is bullshit too. Nova Scotians got a brain no bigger than a snail, ya know. That why they are Canucks."

"You just might end up rich … gold galore if ya listen up good," Thankful said.

"Let me guess. You found a map. That's lame, Lady. Long John Silver and his pieces of eight? I'm outta here." He started walking down the road.

"What do you do for a living?"

"I refurbish lobster traps." He turned and looked at her. "Rebrick 'em and make them good as new." He stopped walking. "What business is it of yours anyways what I do?"

"Follow me." She started toward the Benjamin. When he didn't move, she spun and faced him. "Look. I need a strong fella to help me with a chest. A treasure chest. I can get someone else you aren't interested. You can stick to them lobster traps. That needs doing too I suppose."

"How I know you ain't a lyin'?"

"Oh, c'mon." She started walking back around the house. "Lying? See for yourself." She heard him following her. When they got to the bank she pointed.

He leaned forward on the bank and squinted his eyes. "What is it?"

"Well ... I would say gold. Looks that way, doesn't it?"

He was speechless. He rubbed his eyes and leaned toward the object in the water.

"You big and strong is why I asked you. We gotta get it out. The tide uncovered it, I'm thinking. You help me and half of it is yours."

Thankful kept her eyes glued on the treasure. The fading sunlight broke through branches and illuminated the gold colored bricks. She had no idea they would shine as much as they did, when she was painting them. A tidal wave of good fortune was hammering her. The chest had sunk in the high tide and was stuck in the sand now that the tide was out. Her plan was working out perfect. "It's treasure. Have to be William Kidd's, I bet. Look at it shine. Pure gold."

"I don't—believe—it." he stammered. Stunned. He was frozen in place.

"C'mon. Follow me." They fetched a rope out of the garden shed. "I'll belay you. Tie into a tree. Here." She handed him a carabiner. "Use this."

He was excited. Too excited. All the locals knew the Benjamin had sinks that were bottomless and full of sand. She remembered dead animals disappearing in them; one quicksand hole between the chest and the shore had swallowed an entire cow in under a minute.

In no time he was stepping and sliding in muck. Each step sucked him a little further forward while he got pulled downward. The action of the sand was subtle. After several steps in squishy sand, he started to try and pull himself toward the treasure using his arms to breast stroke. He was not to be denied. "That knot tight?"

The question reminded her to cut it and toss it toward him. She had watched her dad do it with livestock. Quicksand is fast and quicksand never loses. He had grabbed a gold brick, when half a shoulder and his head, was still sticking out of the sand and clung to it as he slid under. The sand self-leveled. A bird started singing.

Dalton's words raced across her mind. She was enraged. He had died too fast. She hated it when cruel people died too fast. "You bastard! No more roofies or picking on the twins. No more sex-shaming. She'll play her viola in the park again. You bastard! You raping bastard!" She picked up a rock and threw it where she last saw his head. She stood staring and tossed another rock. Then an avalanche of rocks. She swiveled in place to sit on the bank; rock throwing had exhausted her.

The tide was coming in. She remembered her father and how they had sat along the Benjamin. The water talked to her and told her she did good. She smiled. "No more using the bible to hate gay people. You bastard."

The eastern horizon was home to the sun. She heard Nolan making his lobster rounds. Miss Kitty Carlisle was eating. A trip to Ellsworth was in order. When she got to Reny's she scored the biggest one they had. A bigger one was available on Amazon but she wanted to do it now. Maine weather is always unpredictable. You could wake up in sunlight and it might be raining come noon. Then foggy before the sun reappears. Today the sun stayed out and was bright.

The plastic wrap wouldn't tear. Teeth did the trick. Then she saw Dalton walking up the street with his five-gallon bucket. He had to get the mailbox post painted for her. After he had painted the first ring purple, she got out of the car.

Dalton spun in her direction. "Didn't see you in the car."

"I have a flag to fly right-side up because it's right. Reny's had one." She snapped her new purchase—the Pride Flag—to the line, and pulled it up over Maine. The flag hung down along the pole.

She took a deep breath. "Life is a great mystery. There are some, Dalton, who feel they alone understand and control the force of love. Such nonsense. It controls itself. Love happens because love happens. You didn't choose the color of your hair and you don't pick your love interest. It's a gift from the universe. That's what makes it special. It is so unpredictable."

Dalton was staring at her lost in thought.

Thankful smiled. "You have to be true to yourself. You can't lie your way into love. You were created to laugh and smile and be happy. Love is all that times three. One plus one is more than two. That's it. If you accept the meaning of that flag your heart will be better for it." She pointed up toward the flag. "Respect breaks out

110

into goodness and all things good make love what it is. I love my daughter and her daddy and the warm path we created together. You cannot make love disappear with a bible or yellow paint. It survives. When people get full of themselves, they get mean. Unfortunate, but I know it is true. That's where all the pain and suffering come from: beatings, rape and wars. Some people get lost in being mean and that's all they are ever going to know. Only choice you have is to lie and be mean—or—to be truthful and loved."

Dalton smiled. Thankful smiled and they embraced. The wind arrived—at that moment—and blew the flag straight out from the pole.

www.ingramcontent.com/pod-product-compliance
Lightning Source LLC
Chambersburg PA
CBHW070757120626
46557CB00002B/638